MW00681777

COMING HOME

Janis Reams Hudson

A KISMET™ Romance

METEOR PUBLISHING CORPORATION
Bensalem, Pennsylvania

To Debbie Cowan, Julie Garrett, and
Patsy Klingstedt

What a team!! Thanks, ladies.

JANIS REAMS HUDSON

Since her recent move from the country a few months
ago, Janis Reams Hudson (when she's not writing)
can often be found exploring the forgotten conveniences of city life—book stores, grocery stores, fast
food joints, and the Mother of All Conveniences,
shopping malls. Yet, as pleased as she is to be back
in Oklahoma City, you will surely realize when
you read **COMING HOME** that Janis is still carrying on an affair of the heart with Lincoln County,
Oklahoma.

Other KISMET books by Janis Reams Hudson:

No. 29   *FOSTER LOVE*

ONE

Only idiots and fools were out on the road tonight. Lacey Hamilton Johnston figured she was a little of both, with "stubborn" tacked on for good measure. Why in heaven's name hadn't she stopped for the night in Oklahoma City, when she'd first run into this late-March ice storm?

She gripped the steering wheel until her knuckles threatened to pop through her skin. The pelting ice severely limited her visibility. *Why* hadn't she stopped in the city?

Stubborn, that's why. She'd made up her mind to finally face her parents, and once her mind was made up, she was determined to get the confrontation over with, *fast*.

Fast, so far, had lasted two long, exhausting days. But the drive home from California had given her time to get her thoughts in order before facing her parents. Spending another night on the road would have stretched her nerves to the limit. Would have given her too much time to think about backing out.

But there was no backing out. Her money was almost gone, and she had no place else to go. Deep Fork, Oklahoma, was her only hope.

The rear of the car slid sideways. Lacey immediately took her foot off the gas.

"Don't hit the brake, don't hit the brake," she warned herself. She shivered in spite of the hot air blasting from the car's heater.

The road looked clear and dry.

It wasn't. At least a half inch of solid, clear-black ice kept her questionable tires from gripping pavement. What she wouldn't give to have her big, heavy Lincoln just then, instead of the poor, abused, ancient Datsun she'd traded it for. The heavier car might have made it up this damn hill without skidding.

It wasn't that big of a hill, but thank heaven it was the last one before home. Lacey held her breath. Slowly, agonizingly, the little car inched its way to the crest. Out the corner of her eye, she spotted a car in the ditch not five feet to her right.

"Seventeen," she muttered, taking a short breath. Seventeen cars abandoned at the side of the road—or, in some cases, in the center median along the interstate—since she'd left Oklahoma City, forty miles and three hours ago. With only two miles to go, she was determined not to become number eighteen.

Maybe on the interstate, sliding off the road wouldn't have been so bad. There had been plenty of traffic despite the hazardous conditions. But she hadn't seen another moving vehicle since she'd pulled off onto State Highway 177 a few miles ago.

She wasn't sure which would be worse: taking the chance of being picked up by a stranger on the interstate, or walking these last two miles home on a deserted highway in the middle of an ice storm. She shivered again. The mere thought of either had more power to freeze her than the car's heater had to warm her.

But the last two miles went by, along with the turnoff to Meeker at Jacktown. The sign ahead said "Deep Fork, Population 1,827." A moment later Lacey breathed a sigh of relief and eased to a stop at the only traffic light in town. When she turned onto her parents' street, the street she'd grown up on, she sagged in the seat. She'd made it.

Since it was two o'clock in the morning, she wasn't surprised to find the house dark. Her talk would have to wait until morning. But at least she was home.

Nothing had ever looked more welcoming—despite her questionable welcome—than the little rust-colored brick house with white trim, where she'd lived all her life until she'd gone away to college.

She parked her Datsun in the driveway, wrapped her wool muffler over her head, grabbed her purse and overnight case—the rest could wait until tomorrow—and picked her way along the ice-coated sidewalk to the front door. With every slippery step, more ice pelted down on her head and shoulders.

Twenty-two degrees, the radio had said. Surely it was colder than that.

As soon as she opened the front door—*Hallelujah, they didn't change the locks on me*—she knew something was wrong. The house was definitely warmer than outdoors, but not warm enough. The house was empty. She knew it, felt it, even before she went from room to room turning on all the lights. Even the garage was empty.

It wasn't until she checked the kitchen and found the cupboards virtually bare and the refrigerator propped open and unplugged that she realized her parents must not have returned yet from their annual Florida winter.

Damn.

She had primed herself for weeks. She had finally worked up the nerve to face them, and they weren't even here! How long would she have to keep herself pumped up for the arguments she knew she would face? The displeasure and disappointment she knew they felt?

Well, it didn't look like she had much choice. She would just have to settle in and wait for them.

First things first. She turned up the heat. Then she put her car in the garage. She would have dearly loved a steaming cup of hot chocolate afterward, but there was no milk, no instant cocoa mix. She settled for a steaming hot bath.

Maybe, she thought, stretching out in the tub, if things went well with her parents, she could stay here. That would enable her to get a job and save her money. What she wanted, aside from making peace with her parents, was to go back to college and get her business degree.

She never should have dropped out. She never should have married Charles. But then, he could be so charming, especially back when they first met.

Lacey closed her eyes and forced thoughts of Charles and all the accompanying turmoil aside. All she wanted right now was to soak in the steaming water until her fingertips wrinkled like prunes and the heat seeped into her bones.

"Whoever you are, you've got five seconds to come out of there."

The deep, threatening voice brought Lacey upright with a splash. She gripped the edge of the bathtub in shock. Her gaze darted to the bathroom door. Her mouth went dry. Her heart pounded so hard she gasped. That was *not* her father's voice!

Clothes! No matter who threatened from the other side of the door, she didn't want to greet him naked. She stood and reached a trembling hand toward the towel lying on the commode lid. Too late!

The bathroom door burst open. Lacey screamed.

A frigid blast of air swept into the room along with the double-barrelled bore of a shotgun. Her flesh shrank from the terrifying threat. She tried to scream again, but nothing came out. On the other end of the shotgun loomed a giant of a man wearing a hooded parka.

Lacey's muscles locked and refused to move. The stranger stalked nearer. Lacey tore her gaze from the shotgun and stared into startling blue eyes.

"My God! Ruffles?"

Heaven help her, the monster knew her name! *Worse—* her *nickname!* A tiny whimper worked its way loose from her fear-clogged throat. The man raised his arm. She flinched, suddenly remembering to cross her arms over her chest. Her mouth worked, but no sound came out.

Instead of reaching to drag her from the tub, though, the intruder swung his hand up and pushed the hood of his parka back until it hung behind his neck like a bowl. "Lacey, it's me."

For another instant terror kept its grip on her. Then she blinked. "Clint?" Recognition of her childhood friend and next door neighbor sent tears of relief flooding her eyes. Reaction set in, and her legs shook violently. She felt her feet slipping out from beneath her. Unable to stop herself, she fell, sending up a huge geyser of bath water. She landed on her hip and elbow, hard, and cried out.

She barely got her sopping wet hair brushed from her eyes when Clint reached and lifted her from the water with one arm. She gasped as her bath-warmed skin rubbed flush against his freezing parka.

"Are you all right?" he asked.

"I think so."

Then the lights went out. The room was dark as the inside of a tomb.

"Ah, hell," Clint muttered. "Stay put. I'll get a flashlight." And suddenly he was gone.

Frigid air swirled around her. She broke out in goose bumps. *Stay put,* he said.

"My Aunt Fanny, buster." Lacey wasn't about to stay put and get caught standing there stark naked—again—when he came back.

She felt her way out of the tub, past the sink to the toilet. But instead of grabbing the towel lying there, she missed and knocked it to the floor.

Footsteps pounded down the hall, coming closer.

In pitch blackness, she stooped for the towel. It wasn't where she thought it was. Dropping to all fours, she patted the floor, searching. It wasn't there.

The footsteps were getting closer. Too close.

Where was the damn towel?

The footsteps stopped in the doorway. A narrow beam of light pierced the bathroom. She spotted the towel instantly, behind the toilet, and reached for it.

"Nice. Very nice."

His words, the huskiness in his voice, had her whipping her head around. "Clint!" He was shining the damn flashlight right on her bare backside!

At his deep chuckle, she ground her teeth and jerked upright, dragging the towel in front of her.

The beam lowered to the floor. "Sorry," Clint said, sounding like he was strangling on something.

Amazing what a little embarrassment could do. Lacey no longer felt the chill in the air. Instead, her skin suddenly burned all over. Even in the dim light, his eyes seemed to strip the towel from her hands, strip away everything—distance, skin, pretenses—until he could see to her very soul.

Suddenly he frowned and looked away.

She took a deep breath, only then aware she hadn't breathed in what seemed like ages.

He thrust the flashlight toward her. "Here. Take this and get dressed. I'll be in the kitchen."

The flashlight came at her so fast she had no choice but to grab it. The handle was warm from his hand.

She looked up to see if she could tell from his expression whether he was as angry as he suddenly sounded, and what the devil he had to be angry about anyway, when *she* was the one caught naked—twice—but he was gone.

Well, never mind. She'd sort it out later. After she had some clothes on.

She wrapped the towel around her and followed the flashlight's yellow beam down the hall to her old room. Ignoring the gown and robe she had laid out before her bath, she pulled on a pair of jeans and her favorite cowl-necked sweater. She wasn't about to face Clint again any way other than fully clothed.

After tugging on a pair of heavy socks, she slipped into worn, fuzzy house shoes and headed for the kitchen, flashlight leading the way. Clint stood at the back door. In the dim, eerie light, he looked larger than life. Grim. Threatening.

Threatening? Clint? Her honorary big brother? The seven-year-old boy who gave her the nickname "Ruffles" when she was a newborn baby? Her own brother's best friend—hers, too, for many years? *That* Clint? Threatening? *No way.*

But then, he wasn't seven anymore. He was a grown man, tall and lean, with impossibly blue eyes, broad shoulders and narrow hips. What the current vernacular would term a hunk. The five o'clock shadow—or rather, the two A.M. shadow, actually—only added to his rugged handsomeness. No. He wasn't seven anymore.

And she wasn't a baby. She was twenty-nine. Entirely too old to feel uneasy around a man she'd grown up with. Even if he did look like he wanted to hit something.

Just to be ornery, and to get even for the scare he'd given her, she shined the flashlight right in his eyes. "Wow. That was some greeting, Sutherland. You greet all the girls that way?"

He held an arm up to block the light. "Get that thing out of my eyes."

"In your eyes is a damn sight better than where you shined it on me." She kept the light on his face. "Just what did you think you were doing, anyway, barging in like that?"

He shrugged. "I saw lights. Your folks are gone. Thought I'd better check it out."

"Next time, why don't you try using the phone? If that shotgun had gone off, you could have killed me."

"It didn't go off. Besides, it wouldn't have killed you. It's only loaded with rock salt, and only a quarter-load, at that."

Lacey grimaced. "I think I'd rather have buckshot."

"Come on and quit foolin' around. We can talk about this later. Get your coat and let's go."

She centered the beam on his chest. "The only place I'm going is to bed."

"Right. With me."

"I beg your pardon?"

Suddenly he grinned. "Let me rephrase that. The electricity's out all over the neighborhood. You've got no heat. You can't stay here, so you'll have to come home with me. I have a fireplace. You can sleep on the couch."

Lacey laughed with relief. For a minute there . . . "Thanks, but I'll be fine here. The electricity will be back on soon."

"Don't count on it. With this much ice on the trees and lines, it could be serious damage. You remember what these storms do to the power around here."

Yes, she remembered. Every few years while she was growing up, one of these ice storms had done enough damage to keep the electricity off for days.

Surely this wouldn't be one of those times. "Shouldn't we call the electric company?"

He threw his hands in the air. "Be my guest." He waved at the phone beside the door.

"What's the number?"

In the thin light, Lacey saw him roll his eyes. Then he picked up the phone and handed her the receiver while he punched in the number. It was busy.

"That means someone else is already telling them about the outage. Come on, Lacey. Even if the power comes back on right now, this house won't be warm enough to live in 'til noon tomorrow."

He had her there. "Do you have the makings for hot chocolate?"

"Has a chicken got feathers?"

"I'll get my shoes and coat."

She left him standing in the dark kitchen while she went back to the bedroom. *It'll be just like old times,* she thought, putting on her tennis shoes. They could sit in front of a roaring fire, sip hot chocolate, and talk. Clint could fill her in on all the latest town gossip. And being the mayor of Deep Fork, he should have plenty to tell her.

With a grin, she slipped on her coat, grabbed her purse and keys, and went back to the kitchen. Clint had turned the faucet on to let the water trickle overnight to keep it from freezing. She nodded in approval.

He took the flashlight and led the way across the back-yard to the gate leading into his own yard. Each breath made a frosty cloud in the air, each slippery footstep a loud crunch as a half-inch of ice gave way beneath her shoes and his boots.

Lacey smiled despite the cold. His footsteps crunched louder than hers.

By the time she and Clint reached his back door, Lacey's cheeks were already numb with cold. She greeted the warmth inside his kitchen with open relief.

"You were right," she said, peeling off her coat. "The heat feels good."

"Won't last long if I don't build up the fire."

With that, Clint and the flashlight left her standing in the darkness while he stepped back out the door. He returned a moment later with an armload of firewood.

Lacey followed him and his bouncing light into the living room, where he stacked the logs and fed the dying fire.

"Make yourself at home. I'll get your hot chocolate."

She would have felt better if his "Make yourself at home" had sounded a little more sincere and a little less begrudging. *He's* the one who insisted she come here. What was with him?

Maybe it was her imagination. She was too tired to think straight.

She tugged off her shoes and sat on the couch facing the fire. The dancing orange flames hypnotized her, relaxed her. Welcomed her. She dropped her head to the back of the couch and closed her eyes, wondering if she'd be able to stay awake long enough to share the quiet, the local gossip, the old, comfortable friendship with Clint.

She heard him moving around in the kitchen, heard the unmistakable hiss of a Coleman lantern. So he didn't like cooking by flashlight. Couldn't blame him there.

Not wanting to fall asleep, she raised her head and sat up straighter. It had been years since she'd been in this room, but it hadn't changed much. She didn't remember the couch and matching chair, but they sat in the same places the old ones had occupied, at right angles to each other, the couch facing the fire.

Behind her, in a dark corner, sat the old ladderback rocker. The sight of the rose-patterned wallpaper behind it made her smile. Clint and her brother Howie had tricked her into seeing how hard she could rock in the family heirloom. Naturally, they'd helped her, and naturally, she and the chair had both gone over backwards. For her trouble, she got a knot on her head from the fall and a swat on her rear from her father. The boys hadn't been so lucky.

Neither had the wall. The back of the rocker had gouged a hole in the wall. Both boys had received a rather minor whipping and a much sterner lecture. Mrs. Sutherland had spent weeks trying to find matching tulip wallpaper to patch the hole, with no luck.

So she had decided to repaper the wall with roses. Or rather, she decided Clint and Howie would repaper the wall. As far as Lacey knew, there had been no more roughhousing indoors after that.

The rocker looked cold and lonely sitting there beside the matching cherrywood table next to the window. Mrs. Sutherland used to tell Lacey how she had rocked Clint to sleep in that very chair, how she hoped some day Clint's wife would rock his children there, too.

Children. Why did her mind always turn to children?

Lacey shifted and faced the fire. Clint's wife hadn't stayed around long enough to give him children to rock in the chair. And if she had, poor Clint would never have known just whose children they were. Marianne had cheated on him from day one. He'd stuck it out for two years before divorcing her. According to Lacey's parents, he hadn't been serious about a woman since.

She pictured him in her mind, not huge and threatening as he'd seemed when he'd stormed into her bathroom, but tall and handsome and laughing, the way she remembered him from earlier times. He'd been alone for nearly ten years now. What a waste.

The sound of liquid being poured was followed by a long pause, then slow, heavy footsteps coming her way.

"Here." Clint stopped beside her and held out a steaming mug. "Watch it, it's hot."

But she wasn't watching *it*, she was watching him. He'd shed his coat. The red plaid flannel shirt stretched tight across his shoulders. The unbuttoned top button revealed the crew neck of a white T-shirt. Both were tucked into tight, faded jeans.

She recognized his belt buckle instantly as the one he'd won for team roping in the National High School Finals Rodeo his senior year. She'd been eleven, and more excited over his win than he was. His cousin Alex, being the other half of the calf-roping team—whatever happened to Alex, anyway?—had a buckle just like it.

She opened her mouth to mention the buckle, then shut it. By the look on his face, she should have made her own hot chocolate, or done without. His frown cut deep lines in his forehead.

She watched as he stomped to the linen closet at the head of the hall and pulled out sheets, two blankets, and a pillow. Without a word, he walked past her and stacked them on the opposite end of the couch.

"I'm putting you out, aren't I?"

He shrugged and stuffed his hands in his front pockets, his gaze settling on the snapping fire.

"I want to thank you for talking me into coming home with you."

"Don't mention it." He didn't look at her.

"It *was* your idea, remember?"

"Yeah, so?"

He still hadn't looked at her since handing her the mug. Matter of fact, he hadn't really looked at her then, either. And he hadn't brought a mug of his own. "So you're not acting like the friendly guy I grew up with."

He looked at her then. Had his eyes always been that blue, that penetrating? She knew they hadn't always been that hard.

"People change, Lacey."

"Have you changed so much, then?"

He seemed to look right through her. His voice, when it came, shocked her with its cold contempt. "Not nearly as much as you have."

Lacey frowned. "What do you mean by that?" she asked, confused and hurt.

He didn't answer. Instead, he swung on his heel and headed down the hall. " 'Night." A moment later, she heard a door close.

It took her a few seconds to realize he'd gone to bed—dropped a cryptic remark about how much she'd changed, walked right out of the room, and had gone to bed.

She raised her mug in a mock toast. "Why, yes, Clint, it is good to be home. Thank you for asking. And thanks for making me feel so welcome."

And she thought, *I'm not the only one who's changed, my friend. You used to be nice.*

She took a sip of hot chocolate and felt a heavy sadness settle over her. *Welcome home, Lacey.*

TWO

What a jackass, Sutherland, Clint told himself. He leaned his back against the door and closed his eyes, waiting for his hands to stop trembling. He'd been unforgivably rude, walking out on Lacey that way, but what else could he have done? He'd been in shock.

Is that what you call it these days? Shock? Hellfire, he wasn't in shock, he was—

"Don't even think it," he whispered to himself.

He crossed the pitch black room and jammed his right heel unerringly into the bootjack, cursing his own stupidity while working the boot off. By the time he got the left one off he was sweating.

"This is ridiculous."

It was more than ridiculous—it was asinine in the extreme to get so worked up over something so inconsequential as Lacey coming home.

Inconsequential to him, maybe. But not to the Hamiltons. Not when they got home and found their daughter there.

He shook his head and started undressing. With the door shut and the electricity off, the room would be chilly by morning. He should get an extra quilt. But that meant going back out into the hall, seeing Lacey again.

So what's a little chill in the air? You're a tough guy, you can take it.

Tough. Right. That's why he was sitting there on the side of his bed in the dark, with his fingers tangled in the buttonholes of his shirt, his pulse pounding in places it shouldn't be pounding, and madder than hell. At himself. At Lacey Hamilton Johnston. At the whole damn world.

First there had been the adrenalin as he'd barged in on what he thought was a burglar.

Adrenalin?

Yeah, okay, I can admit it to myself—fear.

Fear. Right. Heart-pounding, palm-sweating, throat-drying fear. If he had worn gloves, maybe the shotgun would not have felt so slippery in his hands.

The Hamiltons weren't due back from Florida for another couple of weeks. No one else should have been in their house. If Howie had come home from Dallas for any reason, he would have let Clint know he was coming.

Clint didn't know what, or who, he had expected to find when he burst through that bathroom door, but it damn sure hadn't been Lacey.

A wet, glistening, grown up, sexy-as-all-get-out, *naked* Lacey.

He'd scared the dickens out of her, barging in that way, waving a shotgun in her face, but that was nothing compared to what she'd done to him. He was still in shock.

You're not in shock, bud—

"Don't think it."

You're in heat, ol' boy.

In heat. Yeah, okay, he could admit that. In heat. Teen-aged, window-fogging, back-seat humping heat. Nothing wrong with that. Except at his age it surprised him. He hadn't felt such a gut-wrenching reaction to a woman since he couldn't remember when.

Still, that was okay. Okay, that is, if it had been any woman other than Lacey Hamilton Johnston. Lacey, his best friend's little sister. Lacey, his next door neighbors' daughter. Lacey, who had considered him as an extra brother when she'd been too young to understand he wasn't part of the family.

Lacey, the state senator's ex-wife.

Lacey, who had changed so much from the sweet, adorable girl he'd known that she could now qualify as soulsister to Marianne.

"Damn you, Lacey," he whispered into the darkness. "I don't like what you've become. I detest it. I will not be attracted to a woman like you. I will not put myself through that hell again. Not for you. Not for anybody. Besides that, dammit, you're Howie's little sister."

He laughed silently into the darkness. What did he have to worry about, anyway? He'd just been without a woman too long. That's why his best friend's kid sister looked so good to him. What he was feeling, what had hit him in the gut like a charging bull at the sight of her standing there all rosy and steamy and wet in the tub, what had sent his heart racing and tightened his jeans until he hurt, was nothing more than pure ol', everyday garden variety lust. Lust was controllable.

He heaved a deep sigh of relief and fell asleep.

When Lacey woke the next morning, she noted two things immediately. First, clear bright sunlight flooded the room. Second, her neck was stiff. By the time she had oriented herself and remembered where she was and why she was there, she realized she was alone in the house. Clint was gone.

But he'd left a note on the coffee table: "Electricity still off. Coffee on the stove—needs reheating. Help yourself to whatever you need. Stay here and keep the fire going."

He hadn't bothered to sign it.

She kicked the covers off and sat up. The room was comfortably warm. Clint must have fed the fire again before he left for work. She stretched, then winced as a sharp ache seized her neck. Rubbing at the pain didn't seem to help, so she ignored it.

With a jaw-cracking yawn, she stood and tried to smooth the wrinkles from her clothes. "Gracious, girl, looks like you slept in them."

Her voice sounded frail and empty in the quiet house. There was no one to appreciate her small joke.

She picked up Clint's note and read it again. *Stay here . . .* Why did she get the feeling he only wrote that out of some leftover sense of obligation? Leftover from their childhood, from his friendship throughout the years with her parents.

Judging by his attitude last night, he couldn't possibly *want* her to stay. He'd made that quite obvious.

What she didn't understand was why. Why did he seem to hold her in such contempt?

Or was she overreacting?

No. She wasn't. That crack about how much she'd changed had most definitely *not* been a compliment.

Stay here and keep the fire going.

"My Aunt Fanny, I'll stay." No way.

She wadded up the note and tossed it into the fire. Within a few minutes she had the bedding folded and stacked on the couch, and was bundled up and headed out the door.

Sharp bright sunlight blinded her for an instant. She blinked to clear her vision. Then she smiled. It felt alien, smiling. But it felt good, and it was the only thing she could do in response to the sight around her.

The whole neighborhood—the entire town, she imagined—looked like some fantastic fairyland. Crystal clear ice coated everything. Houses, fences, cars, trees, power lines all glittered as the sun shot through the ice, sparkling so bright it hurt to look.

Not a puff of breeze disturbed the scene. If she hadn't been standing in the middle of it, feeling the coldness seeping through the soles of her shoes, she would have sworn it was nothing more than a picture postcard.

Her grin widened and she took a deep breath. The air was clean and sharp and cold. Invigorating. The exact opposite of what she'd been breathing for the past six months in Los Angeles.

Her mood considerably lightened, she crunched her way across both back yards, looking forward to fixing breakfast. She was all the way inside her parents' kitchen before she remembered there was no food in the house.

No matter. She'd get something later. For now she could turn on the oven for heat and make do just fine.

It wasn't until she faced the stove that she remembered the remodeling her folks had done a couple of years ago. New table and chairs. All new kitchen cabinets and appliances. New garbage disposal—the first her mother had ever had. New dishwasher, also a first. Giant new side-by-side refrigerator. And new stove. Bright, shiny, looking like it had never been used. White. Chrome. *Electric*.

She clenched her fists. What a stupid, dumb appliance to have in a house with no damn electricity.

Of course, why should her parents mind? They spent their winters in Florida. Power outages the rest of the year weren't nearly so prevalent. Unless a severe storm did serious damage, in which case the gas was just as likely to be cut off as the electricity.

"Well, damn. Now what?" The air in the house was so cold, she could see her breath.

If she couldn't have heat, she'd settle for food.

But a search of the cabinets didn't turn up much. A can of beef stew, which, if she could find a nonelectric can opener, she would have to eat cold. The thought made her gag. A jar of rancid peanut butter. A tall, skinny jar of olives. She hated olives.

She would have to go to the store. The thought brought a definite stream of panic. She had exactly forty-seven dollars to her name. No food, and her car was nearly out of gas. She'd been counting more than she realized on her parents being home.

But there was no help for it. She had to get food. She fished out her car keys and headed for the garage. The stream of words that came from her lips shocked her, but she couldn't stop them. The overhead *automatic* garage door was electric.

After several minutes of grinding her teeth, she forced herself to calm down. "Think, stupid." A manual override. There had to be one.

She studied the contraption clinging to the garage ceiling, and the dangling chain caught her eye. "That's it."

To reach the chain, she had to open her car door and stand on the frame. Even stretching as far as she could, her fingers barely grasped the little ring on the bottom of the chain. She tugged.

Nothing happened. She tugged again, a little harder. Still nothing. Slightly more than irritated, she gave the chain a sharp jerk.

It came off in her hand.

Could nothing go right? She beat her hand against the top of her car.

"Well, *damn.*"

She'd driven two long days to get to her parents, and they weren't home. Her childhood friend wouldn't stay in the same room with her. There was no heat in the house. No food. Her money was almost gone. Her car was locked in the garage. The air was so cold, her nose was starting to run.

And now, to add injury to all the insults, she'd just broken a fingernail. To the quick.

The scream that came from behind her clenched teeth was one of sheer frustration.

Afterwards, she felt better, but not much. She dropped her head to the top of the car. "I'm just so tired," she said. Maybe with a little more sleep, things wouldn't look so bad.

She went back into the house and noticed it hadn't warmed any in her absence. Still wearing her coat, but minus her shoes, she crawled under the covers of her bed. The sheets were like ice.

She didn't care.

*   *   *

With an hour of daylight left, Clint locked up the feed store and started the quarter-mile walk home. Although the temperature hadn't reached thirty all day, the sun had melted much of the ice from the streets. He stuffed his hands deeper into his pockets, looking forward to stretching out in front of the fire.

The kerosene heater had kept the front room of the store fairly warm all day. While much of his work had been in the warehouse, loading bags of feed and an occasional bale of hay or straw for his customers, the heavy exercise had kept him warm. A simple walk wasn't doing the same.

With Lacey at the house to keep the fire going, the house—at least the living room—would be comfortable. Temperature-wise, anyway. The amount of emotional comfort he was likely to find with Lacey around was in serious question.

Rather than let a blast of cold air directly into the living room, Clint went around and entered the back door. It didn't take him long to figure out the house was empty. The fire had been dead for hours.

"Dammit," he said into the quietness. "One simple request, keep the fire going, and what does she do? She disappears."

He marched back outside and headed across the yard. She had to be at her parents'. It made no sense for her to sit over there and freeze her buns off, but then, a lot of things about Lacey these days didn't make sense.

The Hamiltons' back door was unlocked. He let himself in.

The house was warmer than outdoors, but not by much. The water he'd left trickling last night was still going. This house, too, felt empty.

"Lacey?"

No answer. He started through the house. This time, if the bathroom door was closed, he'd knock.

But the bathroom door wasn't closed, and she wasn't in there. He finally found her curled up beneath a pile of blankets on her bed, sound asleep. And shivering. Her nose was turning red from the cold.

"Ah, hell." Now what? "Lacey?"

Her only response was to shiver and snuggle deeper into the cocoon of blankets.

Without thinking, Clint scooped her up in his arms, blankets and all. She didn't rouse until he carried her outdoors, then she mumbled.

"Shh," he said quietly, holding her close. "Go back to sleep." The softness in his voice, when he hadn't meant to be soft, surprised him.

He carried her in through his kitchen to the living room, where he placed her on the couch, blankets and all.

She groaned, and her eyes fluttered open, a misty, sleep-fogged, grayish silver. A shift of her shoulders made her wince. She reached to rub the back of her neck.

That slight action melted what was left of his irritation. "Sleep on it wrong?" he asked.

"Mmmm," she murmured.

"Here." He knelt before the couch and pushed her hands from her neck, replacing them with his own.

Her skin was soft and cool, the muscles beneath, tight. He kneaded her flesh.

"Mmmm, feels good," she said.

Yes. It did feel good. The flesh of her neck warmed to his touch. Her pale gold hair caressed his hands like the softest silk. The fragrance of wildflowers teased his senses.

The knotted muscles began to loosen. She was practically purring, and the sound of it did something to his internal temperature. The way her eyes went from misty silver to stormy gray affected his breathing.

Her lips . . . Lord, they looked so soft, so warm, so . . . *tempting*. Their shape, the maddening question of how they would feel against his, gave him a sudden, sharp insight into how Adam must have felt when Eve offered him a bite of apple. And Clint knew he wasn't any stronger than Adam.

He leaned forward and watched those lips part slightly. He couldn't have stopped himself from tasting them if his life depended on it.

Certainly nothing so vital as his life rested on his ability to resist Lacey Hamilton's lips. Nothing vital at all. Not even anything trivial. There was no reason for him not to kiss her. It wouldn't mean anything. It was just a kiss. A small, unimportant kiss. That's all he wanted.

His mouth touched hers—barely. A faint brushing, more breath than kiss. That's all it took for his mind to go blank.

Fire. Need. Raw, primitive hunger. All those things and more slammed into him with the impact of a charging bull, consuming him, inflaming him. He took her mouth fiercely, and she opened for him, drawing his tongue in with hers. But it wasn't enough. He wanted—*needed*—all of her. Now, this instant.

He jerked the tangled blankets away and tossed them to the floor, then replaced them with his own body and hands. Roughly, frantically, he touched her from head to knees.

She arched beneath him, wrapping her delicate arms around his shoulders, making him feel as if an essential part of himself, part of his own body, had just been given back to him, when he hadn't even known anything was missing. Then she moaned a deep, sexy moan that shot straight to his gut. And lower. He was suddenly so hard it hurt.

Her long fingernails scraped his scalp, sending a shudder down his spine. He pictured them in his mind. *God, they were red.* Another shudder took him.

Lacey moaned again, and the feel and sound of it somehow penetrated his brain, sparking it back to life.

Hellfire. *What am I doing?* With a muttered curse, he jerked his mouth and hands away. He stared at her flushed face, her closed, trembling eyelids. But it was her lips, wet and swollen from the force of his own mouth, that made him realize how fast his pulse was racing.

She blinked her eyes open and stared up at him. The stunned amazement, the confusion, the wariness he saw there matched what he felt.

Lacey blinked again. "What are you doing here?"

Good question, he thought. What was he doing sprawled on top of her like a rabid teenager? What had happened to him? He'd sworn just last night that he could control himself. He'd obviously overestimated his own abilities, underestimated her appeal.

It was time to gain back some control. Careful to avoid putting his hands where they didn't belong, he pushed himself off her and stood beside the couch. "I live here."

She raised her head and looked around, obviously confused. "Then what am I doing here?"

"Power's still off, and your house was like a deep freeze. I brought you here."

She looked around again. "When?"

"Just now." One kiss ago.

Forget the kiss, man. He tore his gaze from her mouth and looked away. God, what had come over him? And her? Why had she let him do that? Why had she responded as though her very soul were starved for his touch? There wasn't a man alive who could have resisted a response like that.

But then, she probably knew that. She knew what she was doing to him, damn her. Of course she knew. Hadn't she done it before, to other men?

Other men. Oh, yeah. She knew what she was doing, the little witch. He'd be damned if he'd let her think it had worked on him beyond an instant.

The taste of her on his lips suddenly turned bitter.

Lacey.

That sweet innocent girl from next door no longer existed. She'd turned into something else entirely, something he had sworn years ago to keep away from.

"What were you doing over there, anyway?" he asked, going back to the subject under discussion. It was time he

COMING HOME / 29

went on the offensive. "I told you to stay here. You let the fire die, and now *my* house is cold, too."

Lacey struggled to sit, struggled to put what had just happened between them out of her mind, the way Clint apparently had. If he could act like it hadn't shattered the earth when their lips had met, then so could she. She hoped. Just as soon as she stopped shaking.

His reminder of the note he'd left helped restore her balance. And her indignation. Last night he'd been cold, aloof, arrogant. Today he kissed her as if she were the center of his universe. Now he was blowing cold again. Two could play this game.

"Yeah, you told me," she said. "Only thing is, I don't take orders anymore. Not from you, not from anyone."

He turned and knelt before the fireplace to start the fire. "What's that supposed to mean?"

Lacey blinked the last of the sleep from her eyes and ignored his question. She was still coming to grips with what she had allowed to happen, not just now on the couch, but for the past few years of her life. Her uncharacteristic docility, her willingness to always do what someone else wanted in place of her own wishes.

No. She couldn't explain all that to Clint. He wouldn't want to hear it, anyway.

She was saved from having to answer by the sudden blast of noise from the television in the corner.

Thank God.

The electricity was back on.

Clint reached the set and turned it off.

"Well," she said, with considerable more hardiness than she felt. "Guess this means I can go home now."

He merely stared at her.

What had she been expecting? An argument?

No.

She jumped to her feet and gathered the blankets in her arms. At the door to the kitchen she paused and looked back at him. "Thanks for everything."

While her tone was less than friendly, the look he tossed

her was enough to set the room on fire. His gaze scorched her from head to toe and brought with it the memory of his hands, moments ago, burning her with their heat, their urgency. His eyes narrowed and one corner of his mouth curled. What that little half-smile of his did to her heart rate should have been illegal.

She wanted to turn and walk away, away from Clint Sutherland, his lips, his piercing blue eyes, his ability to heat her blood. Heavens, when was the last time a man had heated her blood?

But she couldn't seem to move. Someone had slipped in unnoticed and nailed her feet to the floor, she was sure. Why else would she stand there and let him ogle her like she was some prize mare he was considering servicing?

Mare. Servicing. God, the images that sprang to life in her mind! She could feel her breasts swell at the mere thought.

When his gaze finally met hers, the heat she expected to see, the heat she felt in her blood, was not there. Instead, she saw coldness, *contempt.*

"No need to thank me." His husky voice was anything but cold, yet it sent shivers down her spine. "The . . . pleasure," he paused, "was all mine." Then he smirked, looking her up and down again. "Or was it?"

Lacey gasped. Never had she heard such an insulting tone of voice directed at her. Before the burning in her eyes could turn to tears and further humiliate her, she whirled and fled the house in her stockinged feet, ignoring the sting of crunching ice as she ran all the way home.

THREE

Lacey woke the next morning with a blinding pain in her head and a deafening growl in her stomach. The first, she knew, was caused at least partially by the latter. She hadn't eaten in more than twenty-four hours.

It was also caused by a nearly sleepless night, brought on by the seesawing emotions Clint Sutherland had put her through from the minute he'd barged in on her bath her first night home.

Abject terror, embarrassment, anger, and that was just the first few minutes. Then he'd hurt her feelings by walking out on her and going to bed without a word and made her angry again the next morning with that terse note.

Not that any of those things were what had kept her awake most of the night. It was his kiss, and the way he'd treated her afterward, that had tormented her.

Her own reaction to that kiss was another matter entirely. It had stunned her to learn she could feel that way from just a kiss. It had frankly stunned her to feel anything at all, but to feel so much, both physically and emotionally, to feel as if the touch of his lips was what she'd been praying for her entire life—it was absurd.

She couldn't have felt that way. During the dark hours

31

of night she had somehow blown it all out of proportion. It was, after all, only a kiss.

And on that monstrous understatement, she crawled out of bed.

She downed a couple of aspirin, then took a hot shower. While getting dressed, she smiled. The gentle roar of the central heating unit was such a comforting sound. Never again would she take electricity for granted.

Once dressed with makeup on and her hair dried and styled, she knew it was time to go part with some of her precious dollars at the grocery store. She shouldn't have to buy much. Her parents would be home any day.

Humiliation stung her. She was a grown woman. She should be able to take care of herself, not rely on her parents to provide her with something so basic as food and shelter.

But the simple truth was, she had to rely on them, at least for now. Not for long, she hoped, but for now.

When she pushed the button on the wall just inside the garage-to-kitchen door, a sweet humming and rumbling sounded. The big door raised. Just like it was supposed to.

How about that.

As she got into her car, her stomach let out another loud rumble, reminding her how foolish it was to go to the grocery store when she was hungry. She would end up buying more than she needed, more than she could afford. It would be cheaper in the long run if she stopped at the Corner Café for breakfast first.

When she backed into the driveway, sunlight blinded her.

Breakfast?

Make that lunch. A *late* lunch.

At the end of the block, she turned onto Main. One block later she was parking the car in front of the Corner Café and mumbling to herself. Two blocks. She should have walked. But then the grocery store was a good quarter mile down Main, toward the other end of town. That, too, was close enough to walk, but not to carry groceries home.

Thus justified in burning precious gasoline, she climbed out of the car and pushed open the door to the café. The bell overhead jingled, making her smile. George Jones wailed from the jukebox next to the cash register about a man who finally stopped loving "her" today. Cryin'-in-your-beer music. Lacey's grin widened. *Ah, Deep Fork.* Some things never change.

The aromas coming from the kitchen made her mouth water. Bread baking in the oven; onions frying on the stove; fried chicken to make her knees weak.

Lacey slipped into a booth halfway down the wall, swiftly eyeing the only other customers in the place, three men in the round, corner booth. Did she know them? She wasn't certain, but one of them looked like the father of one of her schoolmates.

Lacey pulled a plastic-coated menu from behind the chrome napkin dispenser and studied it. At the sound of rubber soles squeaking on linoleum, she looked up. The waitress waddled her way carrying a plastic tumbler of ice water and a napkin-wrapped place setting of flatware. She had to be at least ten months' pregnant, by the look of her.

Lacey took a quick breath, trying to smother the sharp stab of envy. *Pregnant. Does she know how lucky she is?*

Before the girl—Lacey figured she couldn't be more than eighteen or nineteen—reached Lacey's table, one of the men from the corner booth called out.

"Hey, Donna, you mean you ain't bingoed yet?"

"Sure I did, Hank," the girl called back, "last Friday night at the Sac and Fox Tribal Bingo Center. Bingoed with a blackout in the fourth round. Covered all my O's and won fifty-two dollars."

"Smart-aleck kid. You know that's not what I meant. When's that baby due?"

Donna popped her gum and grinned. "Any day, sweety. How are you at midwifing?"

All three men guffawed. "Not me, sugar pie, not me."
Lacey smiled at their fun.

Donna set down the water and utensils in front of her.
"Coffee?"

"Yes, please."

As Donna turned away, a high-pitched squeal pierced
the air. The shriek came from the vicinity of the door to
the kitchen. Lacey—and everyone else—whirled to see a
wild, shapely redhead flying from behind the counter.

"Lacey June Hamilton, as I live and breathe!"

Lacey felt her lips crack from grinning so wide. *Who says
you can't go home again?* "Maggie Sue Hazelwood!"

Lacey sprang from the booth and met her best friend
from grade school, junior high, and high school in the
middle of the floor. Maggie darn near hugged the life out
of her, and Lacey returned the favor.

"Lord, girl, but it's good to see you." Maggie's voice
broke at the end.

Instant, hot tears sprang to Lacey's eyes. The lump that
swelled in her throat was painful. How many years had it
been, five, six? How long since anyone had offered her
unconditional friendship in the Maggie Sue Hazelwood
fashion? Clint Sutherland certainly hadn't.

But then no one could make her feel what she felt just
then, because there was only one Maggie Hazelwood—
Maggie Randolph, now—in the whole wide world, and
Lacey was so glad to see her, she couldn't talk. Her lips
trembled; her nose stung. "Maggie," she managed. "Oh,
Maggie, I've missed you."

They pushed back from each other to look and grin.
Maggie's eyes, too, were watery. They both laughed.
"God, girl, you'll make my mascara run, springin' sur-
prises like this on me. When'd you get in? How long are
you staying? Where's that good-looking senator you've
been shackin' up with?"

Lacey laughed. "One question at a time, Magoo."
Even Maggie's reference to Charles couldn't dim the sheer

joy in Lacey's heart at seeing the best friend a girl ever had. "I blew in with the ice night before last."

"Bet that was some welcome home."

"You don't know the half of it," she said, thinking of Clint barging into her bathroom.

"Come sit down and tell me everything. Oh," Maggie said, turning to Donna. "You two don't know each other, do you? Our little mother-to-be, here, is Larry's wife, Donna."

"Larry? Your kid brother? The one who couldn't pronounce Maggie Sue and stuck you with Magoo? That kid brother? He's not old enough to have a wife," Lacey said with disbelief.

Donna and Maggie both laughed. "You've been gone awhile, girl," Maggie told her. "The kid's twenty-three and gonna be a daddy any day, right, Donna?"

Donna gave a proud smile and patted her stomach. "Any day."

Maggie finished the introductions, and Donna took Lacey's order before waddling off to the kitchen. The three men in the corner, who'd been watching all the activity, finally turned back to their coffee. Lacey and Maggie had just started to talk, both of them at once, when a hoarse roar erupted from the kitchen.

"What do you mean, he doesn't want my special sauce?" a deep voice boomed.

A softer voice mumbled something Lacey couldn't catch.

Across from her, Maggie giggled. "Hang on to your boots, girl, here he comes."

"Him, her," the deep roar went on. "Nobody eats a hamburger in this place without my special sauce."

"Well that's what the lady said, Mort," came Donna's reply.

"Well, we'll just see about that. No sauce. Huh. No taste. Must be some stranger in town." The voice grew closer as the man neared the kitchen door. "Why, everybody in three counties knows better than to order one of

Mort Hazelwood's burgers without my special—well, good God Amighty! Look what the cat dragged in," the big, round man boomed when he saw Lacey.

The next thing she knew, Morton Hazelwood, Maggie's father, was across the floor and had Lacey out of her seat and into a bear hug that threatened to crush her ribs. Her eyes stung again. What her own father wasn't here to give her—might not give her much of if he *was* here—Mort Hazelwood gave her, and then some. He laughed boisterously and boomed to the room at large, "No sauce! By God, I should have known. Nobody but you, girl. Heaven help me, the picky eater's back in town!"

"Morton Hazelwood, you old codger, put me down."

"Old? Old! Why, I'll tan your backside, girl, just like you was one of my own. Old!"

When he finally let her go, Lacey took a deep breath, trying to reinflate her lungs. It was hard to do while laughing and trying not to cry.

"Lord," he said giving her the once over. "You're even skinnier than this one." He nodded to Maggie, who stuck her tongue out. "I better get back there and start cooking, before you dry up and blow away. You tell her all the gossip, and she'll tell me later. Good to see you, kid." He gave her a quick peck on the cheek and a pat on the fanny, then headed for the kitchen.

"No sauce," Lacey called to his retreating back.

"Yeah, yeah."

She returned to her seat, smiling at the doorway Mort had passed through. Mort Hazelwood and his sister Ann had owned the Corner Café for as long as Lacey could remember. Mort cooked in the afternoons and evenings. Ann cooked mornings. Always had. "It's good to know some things never change. Your dad's terrific."

"Yeah," Maggie answered. "But then so's yours. I always loved the way he thought the sun rose and set in you."

Lacey's smile slipped. "I'm afraid those days are long gone."

"What are you talking about? What's wrong, Lacey?"

"You mean you haven't heard?"

"Heard what? Your folks have been out of town since December. What's happened?"

"Oh, nothing much. I've just ruined the family's clean record and besmirched our family history forever."

"Sounds interesting. Go on."

Lacey paused while Donna poured them both a cup of coffee. When the pregnant girl left them alone, Lacey sighed.

"Charles and I . . . we got divorced."

Maggie stopped stirring her coffee, and her eyes widened. "You *what?*"

"You mean you really didn't know? My folks didn't tell you?"

"They never said a word. Oh, Lacey, I'm sorry."

"Don't be," she said, waving her hand.

Maggie laid her spoon on the table. "So what happened? Prince Charming turn into a frog?"

Lacey grimaced. "Something like that." Boy, was that an understatement. "Anyway, I'm home."

Maggie's eyes widened again. "To stay?"

"At least for now."

Maggie raised a fist in the air. "All *right!*"

An hour and a half later, Lacey knew everything that had happened in Maggie's life during the past several years. She knew what each of Maggie's three children had been up to, how much they'd grown, and how much they missed their late father, although they barely remembered him.

She knew who had married whom, who had had babies, who besides her had gotten divorced, and how many conference, regional, and state championships the Deep Fork Wildcats—football, basketball, wrestling, track, you name it—had won in recent years.

"So," Maggie said leaning back in the booth. "Now that you know more than you ever wanted to know about the home folks—"

Lacey laughed.

"You want to talk about you? If you do, I'll listen."

Lacey shook her head. "Thanks, Maggie. I can't just yet." She couldn't tell her about her divorce, about what had happened, about what a fool she'd been. It was too humiliating. Telling her parents would be hard enough, if she decided to tell them the truth. "Maybe later. Let's just say I'll never get mixed up with another politician for the rest of my life."

Maggie nodded. "I know just how you feel. I feel the same way about rodeo riders."

"Come on, Maggie, you loved Steve."

"Yeah, and he went out and got himself killed before his last child was even born."

Maggie studied the Formica table top a moment, then shook herself. "Enough of that. I'd better get a move on. The kids will be out of school any minute, and we have to get home. I've got a plumber coming out to the house this afternoon."

"You still live out in that big house on the river?"

"Oh, yeah. You couldn't blast me out of that place."

The two agreed to get together later in the week, and Lacey stood to leave. When she tried to pay for lunch, Maggie wouldn't take her money. Mort had to come out and settle the argument. Lunch was on him. "This time. Next time, you pay or wash dishes."

Lacey kissed him on the cheek. "Thanks, Mort."

She drove the quarter mile to the grocery store near the other end of town. It was quieter there. No old friends to visit.

Wondering and worrying about when her parents would be home, how long her money would last, Lacey bought as little as she could; just enough for a couple of days.

Just when *would* they be home? She could probably ask Clint. He would surely know. But after the hot and cold treatment he'd given her, she wasn't sure she wanted to be around him long enough to ask him anything.

And the thing that really bugged her was that she didn't

know which disturbed her most—his cold shoulder, or his hot kiss.

Which would she get from him the next time they met?

She was sure she didn't want to know. One hurt, the other . . . *the truth, Lacey—it terrified you.*

But was that the truth?

Yes. It terrified me, burned me, thrilled me, dammit.

While the temperature stayed below freezing, Lacey spent the next two days rushing to the front window every time she heard a car, hoping, praying it was her parents. It never was. She was out of food again, and they still weren't home.

She lectured herself about stalling, about acting the coward, about how she had surely overreacted to everything Clint had said and done her first day home. There was no reason to sit there and wonder about her parents when Clint could probably tell her exactly when they would arrive.

She waited until he got home from the feed store that evening, then gave him plenty of time for dinner before forcing herself to knock on his front door.

He didn't look thrilled to see her. She stiffened, biting her tongue to keep from telling him the feeling was mutual.

He raised an eyebrow. "You too good for the back door these days?"

No, he was definitely not in a neighborly mood. She was tired of his surliness. Through gritted teeth, she said, "Why thank you, I'd love to come in," and pushed past him into the living room.

"Make yourself at home."

She let the sarcasm in his voice roll over her. But before she could ask about her parents, he spoke again.

"I never did ask, by the way, just what you're doing back in Deep Fork." He reached for the can of beer on the coffee table.

"I came to see my parents. Speaking of them, where

are they? They're always home by now. I even wrote and told them I was coming.''

"They would have been home by now, but they won that cruise.''

"What cruise?''

He took two deep swallows of his beer. "You know, the shuffleboard tournament? The grand prize?''

Bewildered, she shook her head.

"They won a two-week cruise that left Miami yesterday.'' He frowned and looked down at the can in his hand. "Guess they forgot to tell you.''

"I guess,'' she said softly. There was a sudden ache in her chest.

"But then again, they didn't know how to reach you these past months, did they?''

No. They hadn't known where she was until she'd written them two weeks ago. No one's fault but hers. And theirs.

She sighed and tossed her hair out of her face. "Sounds like you're pretty close to them these days.''

Turning his back, Clint reached for the poker and jabbed a log in the fireplace. "They still treat me like one of the family, just like always.''

Lacey felt a lump grow in her throat. When was the last time *she'd* felt like one of the family? "I guess they're . . . disappointed in me, because of the divorce.''

Clint swung around and stared at her. "Disappointed? Now there's an understatement if I ever heard one.''

Lacey winced. "That bad, huh?''

"I don't know how you can be so flip about it.'' He took another swallow of beer, an angry swallow. "All they got from you was a note in the mail saying you and Charles were getting divorced, and that you were going off somewhere, you'd call them later.''

Lacey turned away from the accusation in his eyes. "It was the best I could do at the time. I knew how they would react to the divorce. No one in our family's ever had one before.''

"The least you could have done, Lacey, was come home and face them, tell them the truth. They deserved that much. At least Charles thought so."

She whipped her head around. "What about Charles?"

"He came to see them after you left him. Didn't know that, did you?"

Lacey shook her head, feeling suddenly cold through and through. "He didn't. Even *he* couldn't have that much nerve."

"Oh, he's got nerve, all right. It takes a hell of a lot of nerve for a man to admit the things he felt obliged to tell your parents. A hell of a lot. Believe me, I know. It kills something—"

"What are you talking about? What did he tell them?" He couldn't have told them the truth. That didn't make any sense at all. No man would admit that sort of thing to *anyone*, much less his wife's parents. Especially not Charles, when it could jeopardize everything he'd worked for. "What did he tell them?"

"Everything," Clint said softly. "The truth."

Please God, no, she thought frantically. Not the truth. Anything but that.

"Lacey, what happened to you?" Clint asked earnestly. "You used to be the sweetest, most loyal girl in town, always sticking up for your friends, always keeping your promises. So . . . good, so *nice*. You said you hated what Marianne did to me. How could you turn right around and do the same thing to Charles? How, Lacey?"

She had to try three times to get her voice to work. "Just what, exactly, are you talking about?" But knowing Charles as she did, she had a sickening feeling she already knew.

Clint swore and shook his head. "Come off it, Lacey. He told your parents all about the other men you flaunted in his face, the man you finally ran off with, leaving Charles no choice but to file for divorce. He told them *everything*. He even came and told me good-bye the day he was here. Asked me to check up on your folks, afraid they'd need help dealing with what you'd become. I've never seen a man so broken up in my life. Proud of yourself, girl?''

Overwhelming rage and horror nearly choked her breath off. No. She wasn't proud of herself, but she'd bet the farm that Charles Johnston was. She couldn't believe Clint—and God help her, her own *parents*—believed that lying, cheating— But obviously they had believed him. Every last lying word.

"Why?" she ask aloud. "My God, why?"

Clint practically exploded across the room and grabbed her shoulders. "Why? You cut a man's heart to ribbons, and you ask why he bleeds?"

He let go of her and she stumbled to the couch, where she sat down, stunned by his outburst.

"What have you become, Lacey?"

How dare he! Shaken, outraged, Lacey pushed herself to her feet and faced him. It was plain that anything she said in her own defense would be thrown back in her face. And why should she have to defend herself, anyway? Clint talked about her lack of loyalty. What about his lack? Where was his faith in her, her own parents' faith in her?

It was like some horrible nightmare, one she wanted desperately to wake up from. The scary part was that she was already awake. She turned and started walking away.

He grabbed her by the arm. "Where are you going?" he demanded.

"Let go of me." She jerked her arm, but he held on.

"I asked where you're going."

If he didn't let go of her, she was going to scream. She could feel it rising from deep inside, a vicious, throat-ripping scream of pure rage. "I'm going home," she said carefully, one distinct word at a time. "I will not stay here and listen to any more of your insults and Charles's lies. Now for the last time, please let go of my arm."

"Lies? Lacey—"

She didn't wait to hear what he had to say. She'd heard enough. With a vicious shriek, she ripped her arm from his grasp and ran from the house. She raced across the yard and into the safety of her parents' home, ignoring Clint's call for her to come back. The scream she'd been holding back tore loose, burning her throat raw. With a vicious curse, she kicked the front door as hard as she could.

The resounding slam echoed through the empty house.

"Oh, God!" Was there no end to the pain one man could cause? Was there no end to seeing her parents' continued belief in that liar, that *bastard?* Was there no end to their lack of faith in their own daughter?

Kicking the door hadn't begun to ease the rage, the pain rolling through her. She wanted to hit something. Hit it hard. She wanted to break something. Smash something! Rip something to shreds with her bare hands.

"Why is this happening?" she cried out.

Blood pounded in her temples so loud she could hear it.

"Lacey! Open the door!"

Not blood in her temples. Clint. Pounding on the door.

FOUR

Clint pounded on the door again.

Somehow, he hadn't expected such a strong reaction from Lacey over Charles's visit. Anger, yes. Even some embarrassment. At least, he *hoped* she had enough of the old Lacey left in her to feel embarrassment. But the sheer rage on her face had taken him by surprise. As had the pain.

If she was so hurt now, why the hell hadn't she thought of that before she started cheating on her husband? Had she been fool enough to think her family would never hear of it?

Hell, she and Charles had lived in a fishbowl since the day he was elected to the State Senate. It was a miracle the media hadn't picked up on her activities and really smeared her.

Still, Clint felt like a royal jackass for coming down on her the way he had. He should have kept his mouth shut. The whole affair—he winced at his poor choice of words—was none of his business. Except it made him mad as hell to see Lacey screw up her life the way she had.

The jackass in him said to hell with her. She deserved

whatever came her way. But another part of him, he hoped the better part, urged him to apologize for butting in.

He pounded on the door again. "Come on, Lacey, I'm sorry. Open the door."

His only answer was a loud thud. Had she slammed another door?

He remembered how volatile she could be. Lacey had never held in her emotions all the years he'd known her. If she was angry, she let the world know. When she felt like crying, she cried, sometimes hard enough to break your heart. And when she laughed, her eyes sparkled, and the world smiled.

And when she kissed . . . he thought, remembering last night.

He tried the door knob, surprised when it turned freely in his hand. Fully expecting something breakable to fly at his head, he opened the door and stepped inside, prepared to duck.

But Lacey wasn't in the room.

He closed the door behind him, then he heard it. A low, sobbing moan. He found her on her bed, curled up in a tight miserable ball, beating her fist against the mattress.

"Lacey?"

"Go away," she moaned into her pillow.

"Lacey, I'm sorry."

Her answer was a choked sob.

"Ah, hell." He couldn't take it. He eased beside her on the bed and put a hand on her shoulder.

She jerked away. "Don't."

Her action cut him to the quick, but he understood it. He and his big mouth had brought this on. He was the last person she wanted comfort from.

But he was the only one around, and her tears tore at his heart. "Come on, Ruffles, don't cry. It'll stop up your nose, and you know how much you hate a stopped up nose."

Lacey cringed. How could he say those terrible things about her, then call her Ruffles and joke about stuffy noses? It hurt. Oh, God, it hurt to know what he thought of her.

She felt the mattress dip, then Clint's arms came around her. She wanted to pull away, scream at him to leave. She didn't. How long had it been since a warm, strong pair of arms had wrapped around her in comfort? She couldn't remember the last time.

He curled around her back and tucked his knees behind hers. Despite herself, she sighed. Her tears were drying now, and she felt exhausted, spent.

"You okay?" he asked softly.

Okay? How was she to answer that? Her parents and her childhood friend thought she was some kind of immoral tramp. Her parents hadn't had the chance to question her yet, but Clint . . . he hadn't even asked if it was true. Charles spoke, the world listened.

Yet was what they thought of her because of Charles's lies any worse than what they would think if she told the truth? Providing anyone believed her, of course.

No. She couldn't admit the truth. It was too, too humiliating. More humiliating than having them think she would cheat on her husband?

Yes.

Clint's hand found hers and held it. "Lacey?"

"What?"

"I'm sorry I said those things. It was none of my business. I opened my big mouth and stuck my nose where it doesn't belong."

She sniffed. "And I thought you and I weren't going to agree on anything. Shows how wrong a girl can be."

"Guess I had that coming."

"That, and more."

He squeezed her hand gently. "Save it, Ruffles. Get some sleep. You're beat."

Something else they both agreed on. She waited for him to leave. When he didn't move, she said, "I'll sleep. You can go now."

"You throwing me out?"

"What is it you always say? Has a chicken got feathers?"

"That's a yes?"

She bit back a grin. Damn him, how could he make her want to grin? "Good night, Clint."

He moved then, but only to sit up and roll her onto her back. The room was dark. Where was that flashlight he was so handy with? She wanted to see his face.

When he touched her face, she jumped.

"Easy." Then he gently wiped the teary residue from her cheeks with a calloused thumb.

The dark shape of him drew closer. His thumb moved across her lips. The rough feel of it sent sparks of awareness arcing into her stomach. But that was nothing compared to what happened inside her when his lips replaced his thumb.

Unbidden tears rose again, and an ache started where the sparks had been. A fierce, empty ache.

Then his lips were gone, too soon.

"Good night, Ruffles."

The sound of his footsteps as he left the house rang in her head.

Why did you let him do that, you idiot? Why had she let him kiss her again? He was the most confusing man, jerking her emotions first one way, then another.

"I don't want to think about him anymore tonight. I'll figure him out tomorrow."

Her abrupt giggle sounded hollow in the silent house. *You do that, Scarlett.*

She kicked off her shoes and without bothering to undress pulled the covers up over her shoulders. In the back of her mind sat the unwelcome awareness of the absence of a pair of masculine arms to hold her through the night. Arms to make her feel safe, cared for. Arms to rely on, to dream on. Clint's arms.

The very idea stunned her. When was the last time she'd even *wanted* a man to hold her?

Her six months in California had been lonely, but all

she had felt missing was someone to talk to. And that someone had not been Charles. No, once she left him, she hadn't missed him. Despised him, hated him, felt repulsed by him, but she had not missed him.

If she let herself, she might miss the man he had once been, the young idealist out to change the world, the fiery law student who eagerly, tenderly, taught her about love. The man she had married.

Lord, but she'd been so happy with him those first few years. The constant struggle of giving up her own college education, working two jobs, being rebuffed by his parents, all to put him through law school, had seemed like a lark at the time. She and Charles had laughed and loved their way through life at the beginning of their marriage.

Even when he graduated and joined his uncle's law firm, things had still been good. They had let the animosity from Charles's parents roll right off their shoulders. Only after Charles was elected to the State Senate had his parents forgiven their son for studying law instead of following in his father's footsteps into medicine.

Yes, the Johnstons had forgiven Charles, but they had never let Lacey forget her part in putting him through law school, thus destroying their dreams.

By the time Charles's first term was half over, Lacey knew the magic she and Charles had once shared was waning. Those exciting feelings he'd been able to generate in her with just a touch had come less and less frequently, and she knew he, too, felt the attraction dying.

But then she supposed it was only natural for the fires of new love to cool after a few years. Such intensity couldn't last long. Yet she had not been unhappy with their marriage, even without much physical loving. She no longer need that. She was, after all, twenty-nine years old, not some teenager in the throes of passion.

She curled onto her side and tugged the blanket up high over her ear.

It was disconcerting after all this time to know she could still feel that sharp awareness deep down in her gut—

physical, sexual, mind-blowing awareness of a man. But not of Charles, the man she'd been married to for ten years, the man whose children she had desperately wanted, the man who had repeatedly denied her the fulfillment she knew motherhood would have brought her.

No. This awareness was of another man. A man she had known all her life, yet scarcely knew at all. A man who had always until this week, treated her like a kid sister. This awareness was of a man who could make her breath catch, make her forget her own name with just a brush of his lips.

Clint.

Beneath the covers, she hugged herself and squeezed her eyes shut. It was ridiculous, having these feelings for Clint, for heaven's sake. She was doing it again, blowing a tiny kiss all out of proportion, imagining feelings that hadn't happened.

She had to get some sleep. Things would be clearer in the morning. They always were, according to her father.

Mama, Daddy, I miss you. Come home, please.

But they weren't home, and wouldn't be for another couple of weeks. She would just have to wait for them. And in the meanwhile, she would stay away from Clint Sutherland. *That* should make her life much simpler.

By the next morning, life, at least in one respect, *was* simpler. All traces of the ice storm were gone. The temperature jumped from the high of below freezing for the day before, to fifty degrees by noon.

But much as she enjoyed the warmer weather, with still higher, more normal temperatures predicted for the rest of the week, Lacey could find nothing else "simple" in her current circumstances.

Her future hinged on her parents' willingness to let her live with them for at least the next several months. She knew they would, but at what cost to her and them? If they truly believed the things Charles had told them, Lacey knew she was in for a rough time.

Vowing not to dwell on her problems for another minute, she went to the store and bought a few more groceries, then came home and started cleaning the house. Weeks of accumulated dust kept her busy for most of the afternoon.

It was surprising how comforting it was to do something so mundane as dust furniture. Since Charles's graduation from law school, he had insisted that no wife of his would do housework. They had had a maid ever since.

Not that housework was ever one of her favorite pastimes, but the mindless task calmed her and kept her from worrying. She concentrated on bringing a shine to the wood, making it gleam. For the rest of the day she managed to put Charles, her parents, even Clint from her mind.

Until he showed up on her doorstep at five-thirty with a tentative smile and a fistful of jonquils.

Lacey kept one hand on the doorknob, the other on the jamb, blocking his entrance and staring at him. *What now?* she wondered. There he stood, with eyes so blue they mesmerized. His hair, so dark a brown it was almost black, was damp from a recent shower. The starched white shirt tucked in to tight, crisply pressed jeans hinted at steel-hard muscles across his chest and shoulders. His boots were polished to a mirror shine.

And here she stood, her hair covered with an old, faded bandanna, sweat on her brow, dirt under her fingernails, a grimy layer of dust covering the oldest, tackiest jeans and T-shirt she owned, her toes sticking out of Salvation Army-reject slippers, no makeup, and smelling like the inside of the bag on her mother's upright Kirby vacuum.

Although why she should care how she looked to him after the emotional wringer he had put her through for the past few days, she had no earthly idea. In fact, she *didn't* care. "What do you want?"

His tentative smile slipped a notch, but didn't fade. He gestured with the flowers. "How about a truce?"

If she looked, she knew her knuckles would be white

where they wrapped around the door knob. "*You're* asking *me* for a truce? After what you've put me through? You've got more grit than—"

"Why are you still mad?"

She sputtered to a halt. "Still mad? Why am I still mad?" She threw her hands in the air and whirled away from him. To the ceiling, with arms outstretched, she said, "He scares the dickens out of me with a shotgun, embarrasses me with that blasted flashlight, hurts my feelings, repeats the most vile gossip about me, and if that wasn't enough, he kisses me senseless—*twice*—and he wants to know—"

"Senseless? No kidding?"

She spun around, fully ready to slam the door in his face, but he was already inside the room, and the door behind him was closed.

With the flowers still in his hand, he gripped her shoulders and lowered his head. "You mean like this?"

Well, damn, he was doing it again. He was pressing his lips to hers, tasting with his tongue, and she was . . . melting. Hot shivers started at her mouth and spread down her body, pooling in a place they had no business pooling.

From somewhere came the presence of mind to push him away. "Stop it, Clint. This is exactly what I'm talking about. One minute you treat me like pond scum, the next, you're kissing me. I won't stand for your hot and cold treatment anymore."

"You're right," he said, his hand still on her shoulders. "I've been a jackass." He dipped his head again and nudged her nose with his. "No more cold. From now on, I promise—only hot."

She jerked loose from his hold. "Dammit, Clint."

"Okay, you're right." He stepped back and raised both hands. "I'm sorry. And no, I didn't come here *asking* for a truce. I came offering one. These are for you." He held out the flowers.

Hesitant, afraid to trust him, Lacey paused.

"They're from my front flower bed. I picked them just for you."

When she merely narrowed her eyes and looked at him, he tried again.

"Look," he said, the teasing glint gone from his eyes. "I'm sorry about all those things I did. What do you say we start over, as friends? I never meant to hurt you, Lacey, I swear."

He still held the flowers, his truce offering, toward her. If she intended to live next door to him for the time being, she might as well make her peace with him. Slowly, still suspecting a trick, she accepted the flowers.

"Thank you," he said.

Lacey smiled. "I think I'm supposed to say that."

"No, thank you for not staying mad at me."

Her smile turned sad as she looked at the beautiful jonquils in her hand. "You know what hurt the most?"

"Yeah," he said heaving a sigh. "I think I do."

Surprised, she looked up at him.

"What I said about you and Charles."

"Not what you said." She shook her head. "What hurt was that you never even asked for my side of the story."

"I know, and I should have. But I'm not going to."

Stung, Lacey didn't know what to do or say. He didn't want to know the truth.

"What went on between you and Charles should stay between you and Charles. I never should have said anything. It's none of my business. If you ever want to talk about it, I'll be glad to listen, but I'm not going to ask any questions. I don't have that right."

Lacey sagged against the back of the couch. Talk about a turn around. Would she ever be able to guess what Clint Sutherland might do or say next?

"And while we're clearing the air," he said softly, "I want you to know that I don't understand any better than you do what happens when we kiss. Just for the record, I get a little senseless myself. But it won't happen again if you don't want it to. I can't think of you as my kid sister any more, but I'd still like to be friends. What do you say, Ruffles?"

"Clint, I . . ." She didn't know what to say. She didn't have so many friends that she could afford to pass one up.

"Just friends, Lacey."

The look in his eyes was what did her in. It was wary, yet almost pleading. It said he meant it.

She couldn't help but smile. "Okay, friends."

Clint let out the breath he'd been holding. *Thank heavens.* He hadn't realized until that moment just how important it was to him that they be friends. Even realizing it, he didn't understand it. Didn't think he wanted to understand it.

"All right, friend, get your coat and I'll buy you the best, albeit slightly overdue, welcome home dinner in town, with a starlit stroll thrown in for good measure."

Her grin was engaging. "In other words, chicken fried steak at the Corner Café, and we're walking, right?"

"You got it."

Then she started shaking her head. "I can't go anywhere like this. I'm filthy from head to toe, and after the day I'm sure you put in at the feed store, you're probably half-starved. Why don't you go on without me, and I'll take a raincheck?"

"Won't do, kid, I—"

"I thought you didn't think of me as a kid any more?"

He gave a twisted grin. "Old habits. Anyway, I don't give rainchecks for a puny excuse like a little dirt." He wasn't aware he'd reached out until he saw his index finger take a swipe at the smudge on her cheek. "I'll wait while you clean up."

He saw the objections rise in her eyes. "Besides," he added, "I'm only a quarter starved, and I get tired of eating alone."

She put her hands on her hips, saucy-like, and pursed her lips. "A sympathy play, huh?"

"Is it working?"

She chuckled. "Why not?" With a snap of her wrist, the bandanna slipped off her head, setting loose pale gold hair that hung to just below her graceful jaw. "Make yourself at home. I'll be ready in a few minutes."

Lacey rushed from the room to get cleaned up. She took the world's fastest shower, slapped makeup on her face, and jumped into clean clothes in record time. While brushing her hair, she wondered at the thrill of anticipation that quivered in her belly. It shouldn't be there. This was just Clint, after all. It wasn't like he was her date, or anything.

Still, she hadn't been to dinner with a man other than Charles in over ten years. That probably explained what she felt now. And Clint's offer of a truce made her feel good.

She jammed her feet into her shoes, grabbed her purse and a jacket, and was barely breathing hard when she joined him in the living room.

"That was fast. You ready?"

"Yep."

They left the house and headed up the block on foot. Lacey breathed in the soft evening air and smiled at the neighborhood redbud trees in full pinkish-purplish bloom. The ice had apparently not harmed the blossoms.

The sun swam low and orange over the trees on the ridge west of town.

"I thought you promised me a starlit stroll," she said.

"That's for later. Thought I'd throw sunset in as a bonus."

"Nice bonus."

They walked the rest of the way in silence. At the café, someone had taped a hand-written "Help Wanted" sign to the bottom of the "Open" sign on the door, and both swung from side to side when Clint reached around her and opened the door.

The café bustled with dinnertime activity. Customers occupied most of the tables and booths. While the jukebox blared an old Reba McEntire tune, Maggie and a woman Lacey didn't know rushed around carrying loaded trays overhead in one hand. From the kitchen, a bell dinged and Mort shouted, "Order up." The usual aromas of fried onions and baked bread made Lacey's mouth water. Her stomach answered with a growl.

Clint led her to the only empty booth on the east wall. A moment later Maggie whizzed by and slapped down two glasses of ice water, then took their drink orders. "Be right back," she said as she sped away.

Lacey pulled the plastic-covered menu from behind the chrome napkin holder, then put it back. Clint had promised her a chicken fried steak, and that sounded fine to her.

The man in the booth behind Clint turned around and tapped Clint on the shoulder. "Hey, Mr. Mayor."

"Walt," Clint said, angling around toward the man. "How's it going?"

"Can't complain."

Clint grinned. "Glad to hear it."

"Well, except for one thing."

Clint gave a mock groan. "I knew it. Tell your councilman."

Walt grinned back. "He's not here, and you are. What are you going to do about our paw prints? Damned sand and salt you guys had to put down because of the ice purt near wiped them out."

Lacey didn't know what the man was talking about, but she saw a devilish gleam sparkle in Clint's eyes. "You think we need to redo the prints?" he asked.

"Well of course we do, man. Those paw prints are a matter of civic pride."

"Good. Then you won't be stopping by the feed store complaining about Main Street being narrowed down to one lane of traffic tomorrow, while they're being re-painted, will you?"

Walt shook his head and gave Clint a good-natured punch in the shoulder. "Nothing worse than a smart-aleck mayor, you know that, Sutherland? Now what we need is a smart-aleck State Representative. You gonna run?"

Lacey leaned forward. Was Clint considering running for the State House of Representatives?

Clint grinned at Walt. "Somebody would have to take over as mayor. You want the job?"

Walt hooted. "No way, man. I wouldn't put up with complaining citizens like me for no amount of money. You're doing just fine, just fine." He laughed and turned back to his table.

So Clint wasn't running for the House. Lacey relaxed.

"What, might I ask, are these paw prints you were talking about?" she asked.

"You heard him, they're a matter of civic pride."

"Paw prints?"

"Not just any paw prints." Clint grinned. "Wildcat prints. Deep Fork Wildcat prints. They start at each end of town. They're painted white and each one is almost a whole lane wide on Main. They meet and turn south on Harding—"

"To the high school. I get it now. I guess they do need repainting. I haven't even noticed them."

"The kids love them."

Lacey glanced at the back of Walt's head behind Clint. "Only the kids?"

Clint laughed. "No, not only the kids."

"And you have to make sure these paw prints get repainted?"

He gestured, palms up. "What can I say? I'm the mayor. It's part of my job."

Lacey shook her head, remembering Clint as a teenager. "I still have trouble thinking of you as mayor of Deep Fork."

"I don't see why."

"Maybe it has something to do with the time Howie held me down and you used a Magic Marker to play Connect-the-Dots with the freckles on my nose."

When he laughed, his eyes crinkled at the corners. "You remember that, do you?"

"It's not the kind of thing a girl forgets." *Like when you kissed me,* she thought unwillingly.

As though he had read her mind, his expression changed. His smile died, his eyes half closed. His gaze trailed down to her mouth, making her lips tingle as though he were touching them.

Other places in her body started tingling, against her better judgment, against her will.

Lord, how could she have such a response to just a look? One simple look. Was she so lonely, so starved for a man's touch because she and Charles hadn't been intimate in Lord only knew how long, that she could feel her bones melting from just a look?

And what about Clint? *Why* was he looking at her like that? They'd made a truce, and since then he'd been open and friendly. A man with eyes that could pierce a woman's soul, with a face and body to kill for, was surely not starved for female companionship. Clint Sutherland probably had women chasing him all over town. He certainly had before he'd gotten married to Marianne.

Marianne. He thinks I'm just like her.

Was that, perhaps, why he kept coming on to her one minute, freezing her out the next? Any woman who would fool around on her husband would surely fool around *after* the divorce, right?

He was still staring at her lips. Uncomfortable, wondering if he was acting this way because he thought she was easy, she covered her mouth with her hand.

Clint raised his gaze and captured her eyes with his. She tried to read his thoughts, but all she saw was blatant sexual intent. A direct come-on.

And gracious, girl, you're falling for it!

Heaven help her. For one startling moment, she actually considered . . .

Stop it! She was a grown woman, not some adolescent moron at the mercy of her hormones. There was no reason in the world why she couldn't just look away from those eyes.

Except, they were so damn *blue*.

Shaken by her response, she forced herself to look away.

Just then Maggie rushed up, breathless, and plunked down the iced tea they had asked for, breaking whatever spell Clint had held over her.

Magoo, I think you just saved my life.

"Okay, you two, what'll it be?"

Maggie took their orders and bustled off. Clint took a sip of tea and looked around, acting like the earth hadn't just moved.

Dinner arrived a few minutes later—chicken fried steak nearly as big as the plate, covered from edge to edge with thick white gravy, part of which was much taller, like a miniature gravy mountain, under which Lacey knew she'd find a pile of fluffy mashed potatoes. Between bites, Clint asked Lacey the question she'd been expecting since her first night home.

"You never did tell me what you're doing in town. How long are you staying?"

Expecting it or not, she didn't know what to answer, how much to say. "I'm not sure."

"You're not sure why you're here?"

"I'm here because I want to see my parents. I've got some plans, but a lot depends on them."

"And you're not sure what they'll do?"

She looked down at her half-empty plate. "I thought I was sure, but since you told me about Charles's visit, I don't know what to think."

"They'll be glad to see you, to know you're all right."

She gave him a wry smile then looked away. "Maybe."

"So, what are these plans you mentioned? Anything you'd like to talk about?"

"No big deal," she told him. "I want to go back to college. I never did get that business degree I was after."

"That's right, you quit school after you got married. You never went back?"

She shook her head, saved from answering, from even

having to think about it, by the gray-haired woman with a cane making a bee-line for their table.

"Mrs. Bonner," Clint said with a warm smile. "Good to see you. Do you know Lacey Johnston, Irma and Neal Hamilton's daughter? Lacey, this is Mrs. Bonner. Her grandson, Jeff, works for me at the feed store."

The two women greeted each other, then Mrs. Bonner tapped her rubber-tipped cane on the floor. "What do you plan to do about the Easter egg hunt if Irma doesn't get back from Florida in time?"

Clint grinned. "I plan to ask her daughter to fill in for her."

Lacey stared at him, frowning. "I'm afraid to ask what you're talking about."

Mrs. Bonner gave Lacey the once-over, then looked at Clint. "Think she can handle it?"

Clint looked at Lacey. "Have you ever dyed Easter eggs before?"

Not trusting that gleam in his eyes, Lacey gave him a narrowed look. "Why?"

"She can handle it," Clint told Mrs. Bonner with a wink.

Lacey nearly choked on a sip of tea when the old woman winked back.

FIVE

When Clint ordered a huge piece of apple pie—á-la-mode, no less—Lacey moaned in mock misery. Knowing how much physical effort he expended at the feed store, she shouldn't have been amazed at the amount of food he ate.

Afterward, Lacey stood next to him at the cash register while he paid Maggie for the meal.

"Noticed your Help Wanted sign in the door. Does that mean Donna finally bingoed?"

Maggie shot Lacey a quick, amused glance before answering. "Yeah, she bingoed—last Friday night over at the Sac and Fox Tribal Bingo Center. Covered all her O's and won fifty-two dollars."

Clint rolled his eyes while Lacey grinned.

"If you're asking if she's had the baby yet," Maggie continued, "the answer is no. But her doctor told her it was time to go home and put her feet up, so we're looking for help."

"I know of several people looking for work. I'll spread the word."

"Thanks," Maggie said. "But we can't promise how long the job will last. Larry wants Donna to stay home after the baby comes, but Donna says they can't afford it,

60

so she's planning on coming back to work. If she wants to come back . . .'' Maggie shrugged and held her palms out.

"Right. Not only do you legally have to take her back, but she's family and a damn good waitress.''

"That's about the size of it.''

"Well, I'm sure you'll find somebody soon. We've got quite a few people out of work who'd be glad for even a temporary job,'' Clint said.

He opened his wallet and pulled out a twenty from the bill compartment. A red foil packet came halfway out with the twenty, and Lacey got a better look at it than she wanted before Clint's long fingers tucked it back into the wallet. She jerked her gaze away.

Outside the café it was dark and cool, the quiet broken only by the occasional car creeping down Main Street.

"As promised," Clint said, "this is the starlit stroll portion of the evening.''

Lacey snuggled into the warmth of her jacket and looked up at the stars twinkling in a not-quite-black sky, letting the air cool her burning cheeks, trying to forget the foil-wrapped contents of Clint's wallet.

She didn't know why she'd been shocked. These days, anyone who had sex without a condom was crazy. Maybe she wasn't shocked. But something made heat sting her cheeks, made her breath catch, her heart go all fluttery in her chest.

Did he think he needed that kind of protection to take her to dinner? Did he, believing what he did about her past, have plans for later? With her?

Or did he carry a condom in his wallet out of habit— just in case?

A hard shiver shook her, and the fluttering in her chest turned into a fierce pounding.

Don't think about it, Lacey. She closed her eyes, then with a deep breath opened them and looked at the stars again, concentrating on them. Even the few street lights in town didn't dim the view. How long since she'd seen stars without the interference of big-city lights?

Years.

"It's beautiful," she managed, hoping Clint would help her out and talk about something that would make her forget what she'd seen in his wallet, and what it made her feel.

One glance at him and her breath caught. The light in his eyes pierced her to the core, singeing her with its sudden heat. Had he read her mind? He was eating her alive. Again.

Nervous, not willing to cope with the inappropriate yearnings he stirred, she looked away and groped for something else to distract him.

"What was it you volunteered me for, by the way? Something about Easter eggs, you said."

Silence stretched for a long moment before he answered. "The annual community Easter Egg Hunt," he finally said. "Your mother was going to handle coordinating it, but she won't be back in time. We need a replacement."

"Sounds like a lot of work."

"You've got something better to do with your time for the next couple of weeks? The hard part's done."

"The hard part?"

"Yeah." She heard the grin in his voice without looking. "We've already talked Frank Morrison into dressing up as the Easter Bunny."

"Morrison? The old grade school principal?"

"Don't let him hear you call him that. He's still on the job."

"You're kidding. I always thought he was as old as Methuselah."

Clint laughed. "That's the grade schooler in you talking. He just turned sixty. So will you do it?"

Lacey thought about the work involved, but that didn't discourage her. She had time on her hands, and getting involved in the community again, seeing and working with old friends, appealed to her. "I guess I will."

"Great! Thanks."

They walked the rest of the way in silence, side by side, close enough that Clint's elbow occasionally brushed her arm. She pulled away, when what she wanted to do was lean closer. The wanting worried her.

He walked her up her sidewalk and onto the porch. "Thanks for dinner, Clint, I enjoyed it."

He stuffed his hands in his pockets. "My pleasure. Like I said, you saved me from eating alone."

She cocked her head and looked into his shadowed face. "Why do I have the feeling that no matter where you go in this town, you're never alone for long?"

He shrugged and gave her a crooked grin. "That comes with the mayoral territory."

"You like it, don't you? Being mayor."

"I like working for Deep Fork, helping the people. When I ran for office, being mayor seemed like the best way to do that. Yeah, I like the office, but there are other ways, more things that need doing for the town, the whole area."

"Like what?"

He grinned. "I'm working on a few ideas."

Ideas he obviously wasn't ready to talk about. But that was okay with Lacey. She preferred his honest caution to the impassioned "help the people" speeches she used to get from Charles, empty speeches, she learned once she realized "help the people" translated into "help Charles Johnston."

"Thanks for taking on the Easter project. Give Mrs. Bonner a call tomorrow. She's handled it in years past and can tell you what needs doing."

She nodded agreement, then before she could blink, he told her good night and left her standing alone on the dark porch.

Truce or not, he was still running hot and cold. She

really wouldn't have minded too much if he'd kissed her good night.

Minded, my Aunt Fanny. You wanted *him to kiss you, girl. Wanted it bad.*

Disturbed by her own inner voice, she let herself into the house and went straight to bed, refusing to acknowledge the longing that ached in her chest.

The next morning over breakfast, she was still fighting the feeling. She needed to get her mind off Clint. What did she want with a man who ran hot and cold all the time, anyway, a man who believed she cheated on her husband? She had just gotten out of one impossible situation with a man and didn't need another one. Forget Clint. She would concentrate on her other problems. Like how she would afford college if her parents weren't eager for her to live at home.

But they were her parents. Despite what Charles had told them, they still loved her. She knew that. So it stood to reason they wouldn't ask her to leave. That meant, if she could find some kind of job right away and start saving her money, college was definitely within her grasp.

And she *had* to find a job right away; her money was disappearing like water through a sieve. And she was out of food again.

On her way to the grocery story she passed the Corner Café. The dangling "Help Wanted" sign caught her eye. In a split second she had made up her mind. Craning her neck to make sure no local police were in sight, she hung a U in the middle of Main and parked the car. When she entered the café and closed the door behind her, she pulled the "Help Wanted" sign down and took it with her.

Maggie looked at Lacey, then at the sign. "What in the world are you doing with that thing?"

"I'm applying for the job."

"You're kidding."

"I'm not kidding."

Since there were no customers just then, Maggie urged Lacey into a booth and sat down opposite her. "Explain to me why the ex-wife of a state senator would want to work in a dive like this.''

Lacey cocked a brow. "The usual reason—money.''

"With the alimony you can get from a man as rich as Charles Johnston? Come on, Lacey, this is me you're talking to.''

At the look Lacey gave her, Maggie backtracked. "Okay, forget alimony. You know the job might only be temporary?''

"I know.''

"You really want it, don't you?''

"I really want it, Maggie. I need it.''

Maggie took a deep breath and leaned back. "Okay, let's get real here, keeping in mind that this is strictly business. I love you dearly, you're my best friend in the world, but I honestly don't have time to train anyone. I'm sorry, Lacey, but I really need someone with experience.''

Lacey pursed her lips. "Experience? I put a then-future state senator through law school waiting tables for three years in the madhouse rat race of a university campus. I think I can handle Deep Fork's Corner Café.''

Maggie's eyes lit up, and she let out a whoop. "I'd forgotten all about that! Of course you've got experience.'' She stuck out her hand. "If you want it, the job's yours.''

Lacey grinned and shook Maggie's hand. "When do I start?''

Clint neared Lacey's house on his way home, wondering, as he'd been wondering all day, what she was doing. Had she contacted Mrs. Bonner about the Easter egg hunt? Was she polishing those long, vampish fingernails, licking those soft lips that tasted like honey? Was she maybe thinking of him?

Not realizing he'd stopped at the foot of her sidewalk, he gave himself a shake and walked on. He had to do something about his growing obsession with her. She was used to big-city life now, fast, smooth-talking men—plural—and money to burn. She wouldn't hang around long in Deep Fork, Oklahoma, regardless of her roots, regardless of her plans.

He was wasting his time thinking about her, wondering about her, wanting her. He didn't *want* to want her, dammit.

After stepping inside, he gave his front door an extra hard shove. The resulting *wham* echoed through the empty house and made the rocker in the corner creak. The rocker he had fully expected to use by now to rock his children.

Yet, after Marianne, he had made no real effort to find a woman to share his life with, a woman to give him the children he'd always wanted. He'd been more or less content—less by the day, it seemed—with his own company. Between the feed store, the mayor's office, and an occasional date with one woman or another, his days, sometimes even his nights (though not particularly in the way he wanted) were usually full.

What was it about Lacey that wouldn't let go of his mind? With what he knew about her, about the type of woman she had become, she was the last woman on earth he should have anything to do with. She had nearly destroyed Charles Johnston. *And if I don't watch it, I'll be next.*

Clint knew firsthand the pain Johnston had gone through, was probably still going through.

But then again, maybe he didn't. Not really.

Sure, Marianne had run around on him. But that was after only a few months of marriage. How much worse would it have been if they'd lived together, loved together for nearly ten years before she had decided she needed more than he could give her?

Clint shuddered. No. Maybe he didn't know what Johnston felt.

He stepped into the shower to wash the smell and grime of the feed store away, determined to put Lacey from his mind. But she wouldn't go. Something she had said the night he'd told her of Charles's visit eluded him. Something he had let slip past him at the time, but that nagged at him now. Something about lies, insults.

I will not stay here and listen to any more of your insults and Charles' lies.

Charles' lies?

Could Charles have lied?

Clint stood still beneath the pounding spray of water. Steam billowed around him.

Jackass.

He knew what he was doing. He was looking for an excuse, a reason, a way to convince himself he wouldn't be a total fool for doing what he had been wanting to do from the instant he had burst in on Lacey's bath her first night home, when she had stood there all wet and—

His hands shook just thinking about it.

Jackass,

Charles hadn't lied. No man would make up something that humiliating. No way.

Lacey had flaunted her men in her husband's face for months, then had finally run off with one. Except for that one note to her parents telling them she was leaving Charles, no one had heard from her until she showed up in Deep Fork last week.

So what the hell was he doing, standing there in his shower trying to justify her actions, to excuse what she had done simply to avoid feeling like a fool for wanting her?

He stuck his head beneath the spray.

When he shut the water off and grabbed for the towel, he paused, let his hand drop.

"Ah, hell."

He had known Lacey all her life. She had been the kid sister he'd never had. Despite their seven-year age difference they had been friends. She had always been fair with him, with everyone. A good kid. Who was he to stand in judgment of her? Maybe she had her reasons for what she'd done to Charles. Maybe Charles had exaggerated. Maybe . . .

"Ah, hell." What difference did it make? She was his friend. The least he could do was act like it. As he had told her, her marriage and the reasons for her divorce were none of his business. If he got hot and broke out in a sweat just thinking about her, that was his problem. He had no call to take it out on her the way he'd been doing.

They could be friends. He probably wouldn't see that much of her anyway before she left town again. And if he wanted her, if he couldn't get the taste of her off his lips, well, he'd get over it.

Then he remembered the way she had clung to him and kissed him back.

With a sharp curse, he jerked the towel from the rack and stepped from the shower stall.

Why the hell had she done that? Why had she kissed him back as if her life depended on it?

He dried himself roughly and decided it didn't matter why she'd kissed him, how she'd kissed him. He had offered her a truce and agreed there wouldn't be any more kissing. And so help him, there wouldn't.

He had some hard decisions to make in the near future that would affect the next several years of his life. He'd be better off concentrating on that than on women. One woman in particular.

When he left the house a few minutes later on his way to the café for dinner, he prided himself on stealing only one glance at the house next door.

The first thing he noticed when he pushed open the door of the Corner Café was that the "Help Wanted" sign was gone. Good. That meant the town's list of unemployed had just decreased by one.

The usual dinner crowd filled the place. The path to an empty booth took him past Mrs. Bonner's table. She stopped him with a touch on his arm.

"That young woman, the Hamilton girl, will do a fine job for us on Easter," she told him.

"Lacey? She's already talked to you?"

"We've got everything planned. Good head on her shoulders, that girl."

Clint smiled, relieved to learn that Lacey was still a responsible person, even if that didn't extend to her wedding vows. "Good," he told Mrs. Bonner.

She arched a brow at him. "Go eat, boy. You look half starved."

His grin widened. "Yes, ma'am."

Clint made his way to the booth and sat down. Before he could make up his mind between chicken fried steak or the roast beef dinner, the new waitress was placing the usual plastic tumbler of ice water before him. When he looked up to greet her, his mouth dropped open.

"Are you ready to order, or would you like a few minutes to decide?" Lacey asked him.

He watched, dumbfounded, as she whipped a pencil from behind her ear and an order pad from the hip pocket of jeans so tight they made his mouth go dry. "What the hell are you doing here?" he demanded.

"I'm trying to take your dinner order," she said calmly.

How could she be so calm when his temper was getting ready to blow? She had no business taking one of the few available jobs in town, when other people needed the money. Dammit. What to her was probably no more than a frivolous joke, to other people the job would mean food on the table, clothes for the kids. What the hell was the matter with her?

And on top of that, she had no business strutting that cute little tail end of hers around in open-invitation jeans, getting all the men in the place worked up.

A glance around the room told him he was right. He immediately spotted four men, grown men who should have known better, ogling her backside. Three of the four were married.

He opened his mouth, then snapped it shut. A crowded café was no place for the things he wanted to say to her, things he *would* say to her. "Give me the roast beef."

"Green beans or corn?"

He wanted to strangle her, and she was asking him about vegetables? He pressed his fists against his thighs and made himself count to ten. "Both."

She scribbled on the pad in her hand. "Mashed potatoes or baked?"

That arch of her brow told him she knew he was angry, although, inconsiderate brat that she was, she probably had no idea why steam was practically shooting from his ears. That brow of hers dared him to explode right there in front of half the town, and he'd be damned if he'd do it. "Mashed."

She looked down at her pad, and without raising her head, peered up at him with steel gray eyes. "Light or dark gravy?"

Through clenched jaws, he managed a curt, "Dark." Then, to keep her from asking, he said, "With iced tea to drink."

She nodded, scribbled on her pad, tossed him what looked like either a grimace or an uneasy smile, and left.

Clint let his breath out slowly. What had happened to him? Sure, as Deep Fork's mayor he had a right to be upset over the unemployment situation in town, but that didn't explain the blinding fury he'd felt in the face of her calm.

You're losing it, Sutherland ol' buddy. Get a grip.

When Lacey threaded her way between tables a few minutes later, refilling tea glasses and coffee cups, leaving fresh water for newcomers, and finally headed his way with his tea, he refused to look at her. He looked anywhere but at her. And again he saw how the men reacted to her teasing smile, those intriguing gray eyes. They stared at her breasts, her legs, and everything in between.

Look at her, sashaying around the room, teasing every man in the place until half of them are nearly drooling in their plates.

No, Charles hadn't lied.

Anger surged through him again. When she refilled his

tea, he barely managed to murmur thanks. By the time she brought his dinner, he couldn't manage it at all.

He never even tasted the meal, just chewed and swallowed. He skipped dessert, tossed down an obligatory tip, and thanked his lucky stars that Maggie was at the cash register when he paid his tab. He didn't trust himself to face Lacey again. He was too angry. With her, with himself, with the whole damn world.

But face her he did, an hour and a half later, after walking the dark, quiet streets, trying to walk off his anger, only to end up standing outside the café at closing time, waiting for her to come out.

"Hello," she said, obviously surprised to see him.

"What are you trying to prove with this job, Lacey?"

Her eyes widened. "What are you talking about?" She tugged her purse strap up over her shoulder.

"Trying to prove the rich senator's ex-wife can come home and rub elbows with the peons? Trying to prove you're just a hometown girl at heart, that you haven't turned into a—" he stopped himself short. God, what was the matter with him? Where had his rationality, his sanity gone?

Lacey didn't stand around waiting for him to find it. She started walking toward home.

"Lacey, wait."

She didn't, so he rushed after her, falling into stride with her. "I'm sorry. I was angry, but that's no excuse. I didn't mean to come down on you."

"Didn't you?"

He stuffed his hands in his pockets and sighed. "Well, yeah, I guess I did, but I didn't mean it the way it sounded."

She stepped off the curb and looked at him. "Oh, really? Then just what did you mean?" The street light across the corner highlighted a suspicious sparkle in her gray eyes. "Why are you angry?"

"I'm angry because there are people in this town who really needed that job."

"Meaning you think I don't?"

"That's right, I don't. Charles is a wealthy man."

"So you think that means I have money."

What he thought was that Charles would have paid whatever she demanded to be rid of an unfaithful wife. But he couldn't say that to her.

"You, too, huh?" she said with disgust.

"Me, too, what?"

"You and Maggie," she said, her steps nearly militant in their aggressiveness. "You both think I'm rolling in alimony from my rich ex-husband."

They turned the corner and started up their street. "What I think," Clint said, "is that you should have left that job for somebody who really needed it. I guess Maggie hired you because you wouldn't care if it was only temporary."

She stopped at the foot of her sidewalk and faced him. "You're doing it again, you know. Sticking your nose into something that's none of your business."

"Anything that affects the people who live in this town is my business. They elected me to make sure things run right, to keep unemployment down, to take care of things."

"People who live in this town? Well, what the hell am I, chopped liver?"

"You won't stay long, Lacey, you know you won't."

"I'll still be here when you're long gone, buster."

"Not likely," he said, "since I don't plan to ever leave. Why not let somebody have that job who really needs it?"

"Nobody could need it much worse than I do, thank you very much."

"Come on, Lacey."

"You think I'm rolling in money, huh? Alimony coming out my ears? Well, guess again, Mr. Mayor. I'm just one more poor slob in this town who needed a job. I wouldn't touch Charles Johnston's money if I were starving."

He couldn't help but believe her, yet he didn't know what to say.

"You think I've got money?" She thrust a hand into her purse and came out with a worn leather wallet, the stitching frayed on one corner. "Then take a look at this." She reached in and pulled out the bills from the side pocket. "That, Mr. Concerned-for-the-Citizens Mayor, is twenty-two dollars. You'll find another seven cents in the coin purse. And that's every single dime I have in the world. No checking account, no savings account, no stocks or bonds. Just exactly what you see here—that's my entire net worth."

Uncomfortable, starting to feel like a heel, he pushed her fist of bills back toward the wallet. "You're right. I'm sorry. It's none of my business."

She grabbed him by the wrist and started toward the house.

"It's too late for you to mind your own business, Sutherland. You've stuck your nose in mine one too many times, believed one too many lies, made one too many accusations. *This* one, I'm not letting you get away with."

She marched him through the front door, whacked the light switch on the wall, and kept going until he stood in the middle of the kitchen, where she let go of him. With a sharp yank, she threw open the refrigerator door.

"You see that?" She pointed inside the refrigerator. The only thing there was a carton of cottage cheese.

"Lacey—"

"That and half a box of crackers is what's left to eat in this house."

Before he could comment, she had him by the wrist again and dragged him out into the garage. There sat a twenty-some year-old Datsun with rust holes along the rocker panel below the driver's door.

"If you want to turn on the key and check the gas gauge, you'll find it sitting on empty. Now you look me in the face, Clint Sutherland, and you tell me again I don't need that job."

Clint felt like a fool. Like a complete jackass. He looked into her fire-spitting eyes and wished she would slap him or something. It would probably make them both feel better.

"Lacey, I'm sorry. I—"

"I don't want sorry. I don't want your pity. I just want you to get out of here, keep your nose out of my business, your opinions to yourself, and *leave me the hell alone.*"

SIX

Lacey was so angry with Clint, and so worn out from standing on her feet for five hours (something she hadn't done in years) that she cried herself to sleep.

Clint would have done the same, if he'd been a crying man. As it was, he spent most of the night cussing himself out and doing a lot of soul searching. He never used to be so judgmental, never used to go around hurting people on purpose, so why was he doing it with Lacey?

The sight of the tears streaming down her cheeks when she'd told him to get out had been like a punch in the gut. One he'd richly deserved.

He'd been mad enough to bite nails when he'd seen her waiting tables at the café. His reaction had been totally out of proportion to the problem.

It was three o'clock in the morning before it hit him just why he had been so angry. "Ah, hell," he said into the darkness. His anger had had very little, if anything, to do with concern for the unemployed of Deep Fork, Oklahoma. It had to do with the way those jeans hugged Lacey's hips. With the way all the men in the place had noticed the way those jeans hugged her hips. With the easy way she had bantered with not just the men, but the women, too.

When that last thought struck him, he cringed inside. Jackass was too mild a word for what he'd been. He was jealous! Not just because the men liked her looks, but because everyone seemed to like her. It was like having everyone in town approve of a woman cheating on her husband, *approve of what Marianne had done to him.*

Good God. He jerked upright in bed. He never would have believed he could still harbor such hard feelings for Marianne after all these years. But apparently he did. And he'd been transferring it all onto Lacey's head. Using her as a verbal and emotional punching bag, because he'd never had the chance to vent his feelings on Marianne.

Good God. *How blind, how stupid, how foolish can a man be?*

With the realization came a slow but sure acceptance that washed over him, like a gentle, life-giving spring rain. He lay back down, letting it soak into every pore and cleanse away the bitterness he hadn't even known existed.

He forgave Marianne for hurting him. He forgave himself for whatever part he'd had in the breakup of his marriage. He even forgave himself for what he'd been doing to Lacey.

It felt good, the cleansing. He took a deep breath, and when he let it out, he let all the old garbage out with it. And that old garbage included the complex guilt he'd been feeling for wanting Lacey Hamilton Johnston. No more old garbage. No more guilt.

All his newfound knowledge boiled down to one simple fact. He wanted Lacey. He didn't care if she had dragged a hundred different lovers through Johnston's bedroom. It made no difference to Clint anymore. It was history. Old news.

And if he was lucky enough to become involved with Lacey, and she did the same thing to him? Well, hellfire. He'd lived through it once, he could live through it again. He'd take his chances. He wanted her. Wanted her more than he'd wanted anything in a long, long time. And the wanting felt good.

What he had to do now was find a way to make amends for his unforgivable treatment of her.

Would she forgive the unforgivable?

He was still mulling over the question the next morning at work when the bell over the door jingled and he looked up to find the subject of his thoughts standing before him. Something inside his chest clenched at the sight of her.

Sunlight streamed in through the high, east window, turning her pale hair a warm, vivid gold, her eyes a sparkling silver, eyes that looked everywhere but at him. His pulse started racing. *Easy, Sutherland, easy. One step at a time*.

"Good morning," he offered.

Reluctantly, Lacey forced her gaze to the man behind the counter and immediately sensed something different about him, about the way he looked at her. Nothing she could put a name to, but . . .

It didn't matter. She was through trying to be friends with a man who turned on her every chance he got.

She clenched her teeth and took a deep breath, then started coughing. No one lacking a set of cast-iron lungs should take a deep breath inside a feed store. The aromatic combination of strong-smelling alfalfa, chemical fertilizers, herbicides and insecticides, and the ton or so of wet cow manure in the small feed lot just outside the back door—not to mention the thick dust of the attached warehouse—was enough to choke an elephant. The smell wasn't all that unpleasant, it was just so *strong*.

When her lungs and throat quieted, she concentrated on taking shallow breaths.

"You all right?" Clint asked.

"Fine." She waved away his concern and made herself step up to the counter. "I was at the newspaper office earlier, and they asked me to bring you this ad layout for your approval."

She handed him the folder containing the notice for the

community Easter egg hunt, making certain her fingers got nowhere near his, just to be safe.

He took the folder, but didn't open it. She forced her gaze to his face and found him staring at her.

"Thank you," he said.

Flustered at the look of—no, it couldn't be pleading—she glanced back to the folder. "They said to call if you want any changes. I have to go."

Lacey whirled and practically ran for the door, her footsteps sounding hollow on the raised wooden floor. Just as she reached the door, he called her name. She turned to him out of sheer reflex, certainly not out of good sense.

"I have another favor to ask you."

Before she could make up her mind whether to ask what it was or turn her back and walk off, the door behind her jerked open with a screech. The bell overhead gave an irate jingle. Lacey had to jump sideways to avoid being whacked with the door.

"Ain't it a fine day?" a loud voice boomed.

Lacey didn't know the big man in coveralls who barreled into the store, but she thanked him silently for interrupting. As she stepped behind him and made for the door, Clint's voice rang out. "I'll talk to you later, Lacey."

Not if I can help it, Mr. Mayor.

But she wouldn't be able to help it, she admitted while walking the two blocks to her house. Deep Fork was so small, and he lived right next door, ate in the café where she worked. There was no way she could avoid running into him—probably on a daily basis. So how was she going to deal with it, with him?

It was an impossible question. She had no idea how to deal with a man who blew hot and cold, who made her bones melt and her juices flow with just a look or a touch; then could make her so mad she wanted to spit—and in her book spitting was the ultimate in grossness. He could hurt her unbearably with only a few words. Sometimes he treated her like a lower form of life.

A lower form of life? Lacey laughed to herself and admitted she was being just a tad melodramatic.

She wished she didn't care how Clint treated her, but she did.

She wished she didn't care what he thought of her, but she did.

She wished . . . she wished he liked her. She wished he would be friendly, rather than hurtful, trusting rather than accusing. She wished he'd be nice to her.

My Aunt Fanny. You wish he'd kiss you again.

She swung open her front door, then slammed it behind her. All right. So she wanted him to kiss her. Was that a crime?

"Oh, Lacey, you're a prize."

She took off her jacket and threw herself on the couch, letting her head fall against the back. She admitted there wasn't really anything she could do about the way Clint treated her. The only thing she could even hope to control was the way she reacted.

Then and there, she made up her mind to take Clint one step, one incident at a time. She would give back whatever he dished out. If he snarled, she would snarl back. If he smiled, she would smile back. *And have him take it as a come-on, an invitation?*

No. That plan wouldn't work. No matter what he did, she would try her best to be polite. And she would stay away from him as much as possible.

The latter proved to be impossible when she left the café that night. She'd made it through the entire evening, dreading the moment when Clint would walk in. But he hadn't, and the later it got, the easier she had breathed.

Until now. She stepped outside, and there he stood on the sidewalk. She had the sudden urge to turn and run back inside, but behind her the lock turned and Maggie called out a good night.

"Hi," Clint said.

"What are you doing here?"

He stuffed his hands in his hip pockets. The movement

made his unzipped jacket spring open across his broad chest. "I came to walk you home, if you'll let me."

Suspicious, forgetting all about her promise to herself to be polite, she pursed her lips. "The crime rate so high in Deep Fork that a woman can't walk two blocks alone at night?"

He yanked her emotional chain with a grin. "Deep Fork doesn't have enough crime to rate, and you know it."

It was a sign of how tired and emotionally drained she was that she couldn't think of a comeback.

"Actually . . ." He looked down and watched the toe of his own boot kick at a dandelion growing from a crack in the sidewalk. His shoulders rose in a deep breath, then he looked at her, all teasing gone from his face. "Actually, I came to apologize."

A hot ache started deep in her chest, but she refused to let him off the hook so easily. After all, he had apologized before, had asked for a truce, then treated her like she was singlehandedly out to destroy the entire town.

"Just what, exactly, are you apologizing for?"

"For everything, starting with bursting in on your bath, to repeating accusations that were none of my business, to the way I treated you last night. I was a jackass, and I'm sorry."

His voice throbbed with sincerity, but she wished he didn't have his back to the streetlight. She wanted to see his face, his eyes.

"I know you don't have any reason to believe me, after the way I've acted, but if you'll let me, I'll make it up to you."

She raised a brow at him, then started across the street. He kept pace beside her. How could he make up for all he'd done? Nothing he did would make the ugly accusations and their accompanying pain disappear.

"Can we try being friends again?" he asked.

The way he said it, his hands in his pockets, his face turned straight ahead rather than toward her, his shoulders hunched as if to ward off a blow, it all got to her. For once, Clint Sutherland was not sure of himself.

"Why don't we just forget it," she said.

His head dropped forward. "You don't want to be friends."

"No," she cried. "I mean . . . that's not what I meant. Friends, yes. I meant, why don't we forget the other stuff."

He stopped walking and looked at her. "You mean that?"

She meant it maybe too much. To hide her feelings, she gave a nonchalant shrug. "Sure, why not? Friends would be nice."

His smile was slow and full. "You won't regret it, I promise, Lacey."

With a mock scowl and a raised fist, she said, "I better not, Sutherland."

The Monday night before Easter, Lacey had to arrange time off from the café to give a progress report on the Easter plans to the town council. She had prepared for it as much as she could, but she still felt her nerves jumping around at the prospect of standing up in front of the home-town leaders.

The Easter egg hunt was a tradition in Deep Fork. She remembered it with fondness from her own childhood. It was important to the people who lived there. Some might consider her a hometown girl, but she felt more like an outsider. She wanted to do a good job, wanted to be accepted. Wanted to feel a part of the community. She'd missed that feeling of belonging in the past years, and she wanted it back.

With palms sweating and heart pounding, she tucked her file folder under her arm and pulled open the door to town hall. An unexpected surge of awe and civic pride welled in her at the size of the crowd in attendance. They didn't get many more people than this attending city coun-cil meetings in Oklahoma City.

She knew from Charles that the population of metropolitan Oklahoma City was nearly one million. Of course, Oklahoma City itself was only about half that, just under 450,000. Still, for Deep Fork, Oklahoma, population 1,827 (1,828, counting her), fifty people at a town council meeting was awe-inspiring. And this wasn't even the annual town meeting, but just a regular council meeting.

The size of the crowd shouldn't have surprised her that much, she realized while trying to find a seat. Lincoln County residents had always taken a sharp interest in local government. They felt as though they had to—if they didn't look out for themselves, no one else would.

An irresistible force drew her gaze to the front of the room. There, in the middle of the council table facing the room, sat Clint, watching her, smiling at her. She gave a nervous imitation of a smile back.

From the first row of seats in front of the table, a blue-veined hand waved to her. Lacey felt some of her nervousness fade. Mrs. Bonner had saved her a seat. It was impossible to be nervous around Mrs. Bonner.

Lacey barely had time to take her seat and say hello to the woman before the meeting got under way. Lacey listened with interest as the planning commission reported that the town's landfill, at the current rate of use (which, they said, would surely rise) would reach its holding capacity in fewer than five years. She heard reports on finances (money was short), on park maintenance (equipment was in for repairs), on the need for a street light out on Old Mill Road at the edge of town, on the need for state and federal help controlling flooding problems along Deep Fork River.

Eventually, as she knew they would, the council asked for a progress report on the annual Easter egg hunt. Mrs. Bonner nudged her in the ribs with an elbow. "Sic 'em, girl," she whispered.

It was just what Lacey needed to be able to stand up smiling. She opened her folder and glanced at her notes, then looked up.

"Everything is on schedule," she told the council, and the mayor. "I can give you a written report or a verbal one, whichever you prefer."

A wicked gleam came into Clint's eyes. He knew she would much rather just hand over a report than speak before a room full of people.

"Go ahead and tell us about it," he said.

Her lips twitched. He wasn't going to let her off the hook. Well, okay. She could handle that. She was ready for him.

"The grocery store has the eggs we need on order. Wednesday afternoon, volunteers will pick up the eggs using the van from the senior citizens' center and take them to the Corner Café, where Mort Hazelwood has agreed to let us do the boiling in his kitchen."

She went on to list everything else she had planned, from having church groups and senior citizens doing the dying, to getting the park cleaned up and mowed. She told how and by whom the eggs would be hidden Easter morning. The picnic lunch was being provided by the adult Sunday School classes from all three churches in town. Mr. Morrison's Easter Bunny costume was ready and waiting (that drew a few snickers from around the room). And the high school band had volunteered to clean up the park Sunday evening.

Clint listened to Lacey's detailed report with growing amazement. Many of the things she had planned for had always been handled haphazardly, at the last minute, by whoever happened to think of them. But Lacey had thought of everything. His respect for her grew by leaps and bounds. She was one terrific organizer. If she had worked for him when he ran for mayor, his life would have been a hell of a lot simpler. She could have handled his campaign with one eye closed.

Of course, she had experience with political campaigns. The thought sobered him. He didn't like thinking about her being married to Johnston. Liked it less and less every day.

He took a slow, deep breath. He had vowed to let the past stay dead. He wouldn't resurrect it. Lacey was his friend now, and he liked it that way. He wouldn't give up that friendship just because he couldn't keep his mind on the present.

But it wasn't the present that had been keeping him awake at nights. It was the future. And Lacey. And something he wanted far beyond friendship.

When she finished giving the most thorough report he'd ever heard, she passed out copies to the council, then returned to her seat. The room was unnaturally quiet in the wake of her presentation. Then a sudden round of vigorous applause broke out, bringing a bright blush to Lacey's cheeks.

"Thank you, Lacey," he said when the room quieted.

Her answering smile did something funny to his heart rate.

The look in his eyes did something to hers.

When the meeting adjourned a few minutes later, Lacey fumbled with her folder and purse. Remembering the look in Clint's eyes a few moments ago, Lacey had a strong sudden urge to flee. A glance at her watch told her it was almost ten o'clock. She would barely get back to the café in time to help clean up and close. She mumbled a hasty good night to Mrs. Bonner and worked her way through the crowd and out the door.

She was being silly, she knew, running from Clint. They were friends now. He had been nothing but nice to her since that last apology of his. A good friend.

But that sudden look that had leaped into his eyes . . . that wasn't the look one friend gave another. It was too intense for friends. Too . . . *hot*. It was the look he had given her right before he had kissed her in her living room the night he took her to dinner last week.

The toe of her sneaker hit the edge of the curb and nearly sent her tumbling. She righted herself and rushed on down the sidewalk. She should have driven, but the night was clear and warm, and she loved walking up and down Main Street.

Voices in the distance told her people were finally filing out of the town hall. She walked faster, in a rush to get back to the café. Once inside, she breathed easier. It was closing time and the place was deserted. She flipped the sign over in the door so it read ''Closed'' from outside, knowing she wouldn't have to face Clint now until she could get herself under control.

It was a lie, because a scant half hour later, when she left for the night, there he stood on the curb, waiting for her.

Friends. They were supposed to be friends. She plastered a big smile on her face and said, ''Hi, Mayor.''

''Hi, yourself. Thought I'd walk you home.''

They started down the street and he said, ''You've really done a lot of work on this Easter thing. Everyone was impressed with your report. You may have talked yourself into a permanent job, if you stay in town.''

Her smile came easier. ''I'm enjoying it.''

A moment later he startled her by reaching out and taking her hand in his. ''So how's the waitressing job going?'' he asked

Her fingers trembled in his grasp. Her palm started to sweat. Good heavens, had it been *that* long since a man had held her hand? ''It's tiring, but I'm getting used to it,'' she answered.

At the foot of her sidewalk, he stopped. ''Well,'' he said, ''guess I'll see you later. Do you want a ride to the park Sunday?''

He still had hold of her hand. How was she supposed to concentrate enough to answer his question when he kept teasing her palm with his thumb?

''If you'd rather not—''

''No. I mean, yes. I'd like a ride. Thanks.''

He gave her one of those bone-melting smiles. ''Good. If I don't see you before then, I'll be ready to go by noon.

I assume you'll want to get there that early to check all
the preparations, right?''

"Right. Noon's fine."

He wasn't going to kiss her. She could tell. But then
that's the way she wanted it, wasn't it?

Still smiling at her, he said good night and left her
there. It was a full minute before she had the presence of
mind to turn toward her house.

Lacey's prayers for good weather on Easter Sunday
were answered in full measure. Riding toward the park at
the edge of the river, she stuck her arm out the open
window of Clint's pickup and wiggled her fingers in the
warm air. The fresh scent of fertile soil and growing things
filled her head.

She felt good. So damn good! She had seen Clint three
times since the night of the council meeting, and he hadn't
given her any more of those hot, devastating looks, looks
that said he wanted something much more intimate, more
complicated than friendship.

No, he'd been nothing but easy and open with her,
putting her worries to rest. She felt the bonds of their old,
childhood friendship knitting back together, along with
new elements from adulthood, friendly, platonic elements.
She felt truly at ease in his company, and he seemed to
feel the same with her.

At the park, Lacey oversaw and helped with hiding the
Easter eggs in the grass, which she had made certain had
not been cut too short for the occasion. Clint had thought
to bring a few extra Easter baskets in case any kids showed
up without one.

"I should have thought of that myself," she complained.

"Relax," he told her with an easy smile. "You thought
of everything else. I'm proud of the way you got this
whole thing together."

His honest praise made her heart swell. It felt good,
having him like her, admire her efforts.

At a quarter to one, the church members started arriving with baskets and boxes of food. Mort took over for her and directed the setup at the picnic tables.

"Where's Frank?" Clint asked.

"He'll be here," she promised.

Clint grinned. "Are you sure? We did have to twist his arm, remember?"

Lacey grinned back. "I told him if he didn't show, in costume, the whole town would troop over to his house and we'd have the egg hunt in his back yard. He'll be here."

Frank Morrison showed, in costume, and was a big hit with the fifty or so children who came with their parents for the annual event.

Lacey watched with envy as mothers straightened bow ties, petticoats, and Easter bonnets. The shrieks of laughter from the little ones warmed her heart, even as they emphasized the sharp emptiness of her own life. She put the sadness away for now. It had no place at such a joyous gathering.

The volunteers had outdone themselves with the food they had brought for the day. Everything from baked beans to giant hams to fresh-baked bread, pies, and cakes, and, of all things, deviled eggs.

It was late in the afternoon, people were heading home to get ready for church that night, the park was half empty, and the high school band members had made a good start on the cleanup before Lacey was prepared to let Clint take her home. She hadn't wanted to miss a single minute.

She bounced along beside him in the pickup, smiling to herself.

"Good day?" he asked.

"The best."

"Everything was perfect. You should be proud of yourself."

Proud? How odd. She *was* proud of herself. The odd part was that it was the first time in recent memory that she'd done anything to be proud of. The thought was depressing, but the pride she felt in her own accomplishments, the accomplishments of everyone who had worked together to bring this day off, was exhilarating.

And short lived. A motor home, with a small blue Pinto wagon attached with a tow bar, sat parked in front of her house. Her parents were home.

She had the strongest urge to tell Clint to keep driving.

"You want me to come in with you, or would you rather greet them alone?" Clint asked.

She turned to him, saw the question, the empathy in his eyes. It was almost her undoing.

Then she straightened her spine. "Thanks, but I think I'd better see them alone first."

He studied her a moment longer. "You going to be all right?"

No, she thought. *I doubt it*.

She was overreacting, she knew. Being melodramatic. These were her parents, for crying out loud. She loved them. They loved her. Whatever disappointments she'd dealt them, however their lack of trust had hurt her, they could deal with it. The three of them.

"Yes," she told him. "Thanks. I'll be fine."

As she opened the pickup door and started sliding out, Clint grabbed her hand and squeezed. "If you want to talk later, I'll be home."

Her smile felt strained. "Thanks. I may take you up on that."

SEVEN

The front door stood wide. Lacey opened the screen and stepped into the living room.

"Well, it *is* you," her mother said from the kitchen doorway. "We knew somebody was here even before we found your clothes. Knew it couldn't have been Howie. He knows his place is with his wife and kids. Had to be you."

Lacey's insides clenched at the intentional barb. No, Howie could do no wrong. Her parents had usually thought the same thing of her. Until Charles, with his smooth words, his politician's smile. His lies.

Lacey felt her throat close. She couldn't keep her chin from quivering when she looked at her mother. *Please, Mama, I need you to believe in me. I need you.*

Her mother met her in the middle of the living room and gave her a half-hearted hug, then kissed the air beside Lacey's cheek. "It's good to see you, honey."

While it wasn't the loving greeting Lacey had hoped for, it was better than the one she had feared. She slumped with relief. "It's good to see you, too, Mama."

Irma patted her awkwardly, then pulled back. "Let me look at you, honey." Over her shoulder, she hollered, "Neal, Lacey's here!"

"Hey, sugarpie," her dad called. An instant later he stepped in from the garage, took her from her mother's side and nearly cracked her ribs in a bear hug. Lacey blinked to clear her vision. Her father would never contradict her mother. He had always steadfastly refused to take sides in their frequent clashes over the years. It seemed Lacey and her mother hadn't agreed on much since Lacey was in the ninth grade. Still, her daddy always managed to let Lacey know how much he loved her. She hugged him back.

"Where'd all that scrap metal in the garage come from?" he demanded.

Lacey looked at him, confused. "Scrap metal?"

"Yeah, on wheels."

She gave him a mock glare. "Don't insult my car that way." To both of them she said, "Did you get my letter saying I was coming?"

Neal released her and Irma answered, "Got it the day we got off the cruise ship. We tried to call you a couple of times when we stopped for the night on our way home, to let you know we were coming, but you never answered."

"I was probably at work."

Irma raised a gray eyebrow. "Work?"

"I have a part-time job."

Neal cleared his throat. "I'll let you two girls hash this out. I've got a motor home to unload."

Now why should her father suddenly look uneasy? A tingle of warning tickled the back of Lacey's neck.

When he was out the door, Irma spoke sharply. "So, are you ready to go back?"

Wary at the sudden change in tone, Lacey said, "Back? Back where?"

"Don't fool with me, honey," Irma said in that voice that meant "I'm on to you and your tricks."

The narrowed eyes set off alarm bells in Lacey's mind. She knew what was coming, just as sure as anything.

"I mean," her mother said, "are you ready to go back to your husband, where you belong?"

What little euphoria Lacey might have felt died a swift death. "I understand he came to see you."

"Which is more than I can say for our own daughter." Irma crossed her arms over her ample bosom and turned half away. "But then, after what you did, I can see how you maybe wouldn't want to face your father and me."

"Mama, you can't—"

"Where did we go wrong, Lacey June? Your father and I raised you the best we knew how. You were always such a good girl, and now this. You certainly didn't learn that kind of thing at home."

Betrayal, sharp and white-hot, sliced through Lacey. *Don't scream, Lacey. Stay calm.* She clenched her fists at her sides. "Remember the time Barbie Samuels's mother came over from next door and told you I had pushed Barbie into a mud puddle?"

"What's that got to do—"

"Remember what you said to her?"

"No, I don't, and it's beside the point."

"No, Mama, it *is* the point. You looked down at Barbie, all covered in mud, and told Mrs. Samuels that you knew your daughter better than that, you knew I wouldn't have done such a thing."

"So?"

"I had mud on me, too, but you didn't even ask me what happened. You trusted me, had faith in me, and stood up for me, no questions asked."

"We're not talking about a little-girl stunt here. We're talking about you and Charles, about your marriage, your whole life."

"We're talking about why you would listen to the things Charles told you, the lies, and not have the same kind of faith in me you used to have, when it's so much more important now."

"Lies?" Irma's chin tucked in on itself. "What lies?"

"All of it," Lacey cried. "Everything he told you that day was a lie."

Irma drew back, her eyes wide. "Lacey June, I'm ashamed of you. I can't believe you would call your own husband a liar."

"He's not my husband!"

"He'd still be your husband if you would straighten up. Charles wouldn't lie and you know it. Not about something like this."

"But I would, is that it?"

Irma shook her head and sighed, not looking Lacey in the eye. "I don't really blame you for lying, honey. It's a terrible thing you've done. But I guess if I were you, I wouldn't admit it either. Do you have any idea how bad you've hurt your own husband?"

Lacey ground her teeth together. "He's not my husband," she said slowly, firmly. "Not anymore."

"And whose fault is that?" Irma flung a hand in the air. "You've brought disgrace down on our family and his. How are you going to live with that? How are *we* going to live with it? Your father was postmaster of this town for thirty years . . ."

Lacey fumed. Here it came again. That speech about how the Hamiltons had to hold themselves above the rest of the community, had to set an example. People looked up to them. The Hamiltons must always be at their best in the way they dressed, the way they spoke, the way they lived their lives.

Her mother went through the whole routine. Lacey could have recited it with her word for word, she'd heard it so many times over the years. But this time her mother didn't stop with the usual speech.

"Charles Johnston was the best thing that ever happened to you, and you know it," Irma said emphatically. "He's *somebody*. He's rich and important. How could you do such a thing to a fine man like him? If you'd listened to me and given that poor man the children he needed, wanted, you wouldn't have had time to do this unspeakable—''

Something snapped inside Lacey. The mention of children was the final straw. Without letting her mother finish, Lacey spoke.

''I don't know why I'm bothering, but I'm going to say this one time. Charles is the one who never wanted children, Mama, not me. I begged him, and he always said the time wasn't right. When he told you otherwise, he lied. And he lied when he came to see you this last time, too. Clint told me all about it. I did not run around on Charles. I can't believe you'd think I would. I thought you knew me better than that.''

''Charles said you would deny it.''

''Yes,'' Lacey said, suddenly exhausted, heartsick beyond endurance. ''I imagine he did.''

From outside, she heard her father shout a greeting. Clint shouted back. A moment later she heard the two men in conversation out by the curb. She couldn't work up enough energy to wonder what they said to each other.

Irma started in on her again. ''You can't expect me to believe a man would make up such a humiliating story. You just can't expect me to believe it.''

''But I do expect it, Mama.'' She walked away and left Irma sputtering.

Lacey closed her bedroom door and leaned against it with her eyes closed. It hurt. God, how it hurt. This was worse, a thousand times worse than what she'd felt when Clint had accused her of the same things her mother just had.

She had a startling urge to run next door and curl up in Clint's arms for safety. Clint, the one who had first brought her this pain.

The whole idea was, of course, ridiculous. She didn't need Clint at all, much less to keep her safe from her own parents.

Why? Why would her parents believe Charles?

But then they had always believed Charles, and Lacey

knew she had let them. That was a mistake she was now paying for. Maybe if she had set them straight years ago, they wouldn't be so ready to jump to Charles's defense. But he had been her husband, and she had loved him. Or rather, she had loved the man she'd thought he was. It would have been intolerable to tell her parents truths that would have made them dislike their son-in-law.

Yet, when Lacey had begun to realize what she was doing, making excuses so she wouldn't have to face the kind of man Charles really was, she had done nothing. Nothing but bury her head in the sand. Like a coward.

She should have handled things differently that day three years ago, when the lies had first come to light, when Lacey had first realized what kind of man Charles really was.

She and Charles had come bearing gifts on Christmas afternoon. Christmas Eve and Christmas morning were always spent with his family. That, too, she should never have accepted so docilely. That, and so many other things.

With her eyes closed, the scene played out vividly. Wrapping paper and bows tossed haphazardly to the floor. The whole family, including Howie, his wife and three children, Lacey's parents, and Charles and herself, had gathered around the Christmas tree, all of them groaning from having eaten too much. Presents had been examined, tried on, played with. The kids had been oohing and ahing over the expensive toys she and Charles had brought them.

"When are you two going to stop spending so much on other people's children," Irma had questioned—she frequently complained that Lacey and Charles were always too extravagant—"and start a family of your own?"

A deep ache had started in Lacey's chest. She had looked at Charles, certain that her longing showed on her face. She remembered the shock she had felt at seeing the same longing in Charles's eyes. For one brief moment, she had thought—

Then Charles had spoken. "I've thought the same thing for years—"

Lacey's stomach had clenched with outrage.

"But Lacey has convinced me that I'm home so little, because of my practice and the senate, it really wouldn't be fair. She's made me see the timing just isn't right yet."

"Charles! How can you—"

"It's all right, darling," he had said with that whipped puppy look she'd come just then to realize was totally calculating. "I know you're right. It's just a little hard to accept sometimes. Especially on days like this."

Lacey's parents, along with Howie and Becky, had frowned at Lacey the rest of the day. Once she and Charles were in the car on their way home, she had let loose.

"How dare you say such an outrageous thing to my family!"

"Calm down, darling," he had said. "Your parents don't always have enough faith in you. I was just trying to help them realize how smart and practical you are."

Lord help her, she had let him talk her out of being mad. He was good at that. He'd always been able to convince her black was white. She should have left him then. Before things had gotten so much worse. Irreparably worse. Before he had managed to strip away all traces of her dignity and self-esteem.

But no, Lacey-the-Doormat had given in, stayed with him, and begged for more.

Stupid, stupid, stupid.

She had let Charles lie to her parents for years. Heaven help her, she had even lied for him. Now, when his lies had grown monstrous, how could she convince them of the truth?

What have you done to your life, Lacey?

"Screwed it up, that's what," she whispered sadly.

Knowing she couldn't hide in her room forever, she finally left its relative safety.

Her mother was cooking dinner. "Can I help?" Lacey asked.

Without looking, Irma replied, "You can set the table."

Over dinner, neither of her parents would look at her.

Her mother had obviously told her father about their earlier conversation. The tension in the room was thicker than Irma's gravy.

After filling and emptying his plate twice, Neal laid his fork down. "Mama tells me you've got a job here in town."

"Yes," Lacey said, thinking this topic was better than nothing. "I'm working evenings at the Corner Café. I'm off Wednesdays and Sundays, but they're closed today for Easter anyway."

"Does that mean Donna had her baby?" Irma asked, starting to stack plates.

"Not yet, but any day."

"So if you've got a job, I guess you didn't just come for a visit, am I right?" her dad asked.

The tension in the air thickened, sharpened.

Lacey took a deep breath. "No, I didn't. I was wondering . . ." Lord, it shouldn't have been so hard, she knew. But it was, and it didn't look like it was going to get easier. *Just say it, Lacey.* "I was wondering, well, that is, I'd like to go back to college and get my business degree. Oklahoma Baptist University in Shawnee has a good program. I was wondering . . . if you'd mind if I lived here for a while. I don't think I can afford to pay rent and go to school both."

There. She had done it. Now it was up to them.

The only sound in the room was the occasional gurgle of the coffee maker on the cabinet behind Lacey. Even Irma had stopped clattering the dishes. She and Neal stared at Lacey in apparent shock. The silence stretched, the tension built, until Lacey thought she might scream. Instead, she said, "Well, what do you think? Can I stay here?"

Her father glanced at her mother, then took a sip of coffee. He set the cup back on its saucer with exaggerated care. "You know what we think you should do."

"Yes." She knew, but she didn't want to hear him say it, didn't want him or her mother to talk about Charles.

"I know what you want, but believe me, it's not going to happen. Can I stay here?"

Irma heaved a sigh. "Of course you can stay here. You're our daughter. We wouldn't turn you away, you know that. But we both think you're making the biggest mistake of your life. Why you'd want to waste your time and money on college at your age is beyond me. Most of the men there are too young for you. I know Charles still loves you. He'd take you back in a minute, if you'd only ask him."

"Mama—"

"Lacey, you should have seen him when he was here. Why, I've never known a man could be so broken up. I can't believe you don't understand how badly you hurt him. What was it you saw in those other men that Charles couldn't give you?"

"Mama, there *were* no other men!"

"I told you she'd just deny it," Irma said sadly to Neal. "Didn't I? I told you. But like I told her, I'd deny something that shameful, too. I'd never want to admit it to a living soul."

"This isn't going to work," Lacey told them. She scooted her chair back and stood. "I'll find someplace else to live." She started around the table, but Neal caught her hand.

"Now hold on, sugarpie."

Sharp pain knifed her belly. Why did he have to call her by that pet name? That's what he'd called her when he loved her, trusted her, had faith in her. While he might still love her—he was, after all, her father—the trust and faith had somehow gotten lost over the years.

No, not lost, just transferred from her to Charles.

"If you're not ready to go back to your husband—"

"He's not my husband, and I'll *never* go back to him."

Neal pressed his lips together and frowned. Irma set a stack of plates in the sink with undo clatter. Over her shoulder, she said, "Let's keep a civil tongue in our head, honey. What your daddy's trying to say is, you can stay here as long as you need to, until you get your life straightened out again.''

You mean until I come to my senses and go back to Charles, Lacey thought. But she bit her tongue on the words. Instead, she nodded. ''Thank you.'' She pulled her hand from Neal's and went to help her mother clean up the kitchen. The two women spoke only when necessary, but the activity helped disperse some of the tension.

The quiet was getting to Clint. He turned on the television, flipped through the channels, then turned it off again.

What was going on next door? How was Lacey dealing with her parents? Were they being as hard on her as he himself had been? The idea made him wince.

He stuffed his hands into his pockets and stifled the urge to rush over there to Lacey's defense. He didn't care what she'd done to her ex-husband. He didn't want Mr. and Mrs. H. picking on her, upsetting her, making her cry.

''You're a fine one to talk,'' he said aloud. ''You made her cry.''

Yes. He had flung his accusations, repeated Charles's tale, and made her cry. But he and Lacey had gotten beyond that. She had forgiven him. She seemed at ease with him these past few days. He didn't want anything to disrupt that.

He wanted to be able to protect her, keep her from being hurt, by her parents, by anyone. He wanted to touch her, kiss her, make her forget the other men in her life. Wanted her to touch him, kiss him, want only him.

Not the stuff of simple friendship.

When Lacey went to work the next afternoon, the café was empty except for Maggie and Mort. Lacey inhaled. *Ahh.* Today's special was spaghetti.

Maggie had a half hour before her kids would be out of school, so she talked Lacey into sitting down for a glass of tea. ''I hear your parents are home,'' Maggie said.

"Yes. They were at the house when I got home from the park yesterday."

"I'll bet they were exhausted. Did they have a good trip?"

Lacey gave a wry smile. "We never got around to that."

Maggie sat back and frowned. "Anything you want to talk about?"

Lacey might have, if she'd thought it would have helped anything. But Maggie had her hands full raising three fatherless children. She didn't need to carry around Lacey's troubles, and Lacey knew Maggie would do just that. "No," she said. "I just have to grit my teeth until things calm down."

"Your mother ragging you about your divorce?"

Lacey grimaced and nodded.

Maggie slapped the table and grinned. "Well, if things get too bad, there's always the apartment out back."

"Over the garage in the alley? The garage that looks like it's about to collapse?"

Maggie grinned. "That's the one."

"Gee, thanks."

"No kidding." Maggie dropped her grin. "If your mom gets too much for you, or you decide you need some privacy, the keys are under the cash tray in the register. The apartment is certainly no decorator showplace, but it's clean. And private. I know I couldn't go home and live with my mother again, and she's not even mad at me."

"That's because you haven't singlehandedly destroyed the entire family's reputation by divorcing the most wonderful man in the whole wide world."

The two talked a few more minutes, then Maggie left for the day. Harriet, the other evening waitress, came in at four-thirty, followed by several customers. As the afternoon progressed, the lift Maggie had given Lacey faded. Depression set back in and affected her work. She screwed up orders, spilled coffee (at least it was on the counter instead of on a customer), and mixed up two tickets.

All in all, not one of her better days.

Then Clint walked through the door. Clint, the first one to bring her the pain of Charles' lies. Clint, the man who thought the same as her parents. The pain in her chest deepened.

When she placed a glass of water on his table, he took her hand. "How did it go yesterday with your folks?"

She heard the caring in his voice, saw it in his eyes. The pain ebbed and she was able to smile. "Not well."

He squeezed her hand. "You okay?"

"Yeah, I'm okay." And with the words, she was. The soft look in his eyes didn't hurt any, either. "You can let go of my hand now," she told him.

"And if I'm not ready to let go?"

"Clint." She tugged gently, but he held on. "People are starting to stare."

"So? Let them."

Her pulse quickened. "Clint, let go."

"Say please."

"Please."

He grinned. "Anything you say." And he let go.

She had trouble fighting back an answering grin and controlling her racing heart. Just from his touch.

From that point, the evening improved. She quit dwelling on the problem with her parents and was able to concentrate on her job and enjoy herself. And remember the warmth and strength of a man's work-hardened hand on hers.

When Mort locked the door behind her at ten-thirty and she turned toward the street, her insides tingled. Clint was there, waiting for her. This time, instead of standing on the sidewalk with his hands in his hip pockets, he lounged against the hood of his pickup, elbows braced behind him, one foot crossed negligently over the other. He looked suddenly taller, his shoulders broader, hips leaner, legs longer. His eyes, hotter.

With a cocky grin, he pulled the toothpick from the

corner of his mouth and tucked it into his shirt pocket. "Hi."

Maybe she'd only imagined the heat in his eyes. Now they held some emotion she couldn't identify. She took a quick breath to steady her voice. "Hi." She looked to his pickup, then back at him, in question.

"Thought you could use a diversion tonight. How about a ride?"

She hadn't realized how much she'd been dreading going home until he offered her this chance to delay it. "Sure. Where to?"

"It's a beautiful, moonlit night." He opened the passenger door for her, ushered her in, and closed it behind her. "I thought a ride in the country along some dark, deserted road might be nice."

Her heart started thumping. She narrowed her eyes and watched him walk around and get in through the driver's door. "Moonlight?" she said. "A ride in the country, a deserted road? I thought this was a *friendship*."

He started the truck and have her an innocent look. "We're friends, aren't we?"

"I'm just trying to make sure we stay that way."

"You're too suspicious." He backed out of the parking space and headed south on Main toward the river at the edge of town. "I'm talking *friendly* moonlight, *friendly* country, a nice, quiet, *friendly* deserted road."

Friendly or not, Lacey's heart raced anyway.

They left the town and its lights behind and drove through the steel framework of the old bridge across the Deep Fork River. Clint turned off onto what was little more than a cow path that followed the north bank. He told himself to slow down. And he wasn't thinking about his driving speed.

He'd nearly scared her off back there with talk of moonlight and dark country roads. She didn't need more complications in her life right now, he knew. She was hurt, vulnerable.

And he wanted her like hell.

But he didn't want to push, and he didn't want her to turn to him only for comfort. He wanted her to come to him when her mind was free and clear, when she wasn't preoccupied with something else, when her only thought was how much she wanted him.

And she did want him. Or she had those few times he'd kissed her. She would again.

But not tonight. Tonight she needed peace. She need to laugh and forget, to think of something else. He knew what he wanted her to think about, but that brought him back full circle. He wanted her to think about him. Nice thoughts. Good thoughts. *Hot* thoughts.

He hit a pothole that tossed him and Lacey nearly through the roof. "Sorry," he muttered. Time to get his mind off Lacey and on his driving, before he did something stupid like crash into a tree. He glanced over and saw her hanging on to the arm rest, trying not to laugh.

He pulled the pickup into the next clearing alongside the river and killed the engine. Lacey released her grip on the arm rest and rolled down her window.

"Whew! If that's your idea of a friendly ride, I'm glad you're not mad at me."

Moonlight streamed across her shoulder and down her chest, leaving her face in shadow. The easy rustling of water meandering past and the wind whispering through newly leafed trees were nearly drowned out by the vibrant chorus of singing toads.

Lacey leaned toward him. He turned to face her, keeping one arm draped across the steering wheel. It was that, he knew, or wrap both his arms around her.

"You're not mad at me are you?" she asked.

Clint tried to still the longing in his gut. "Of course not."

"Then what's wrong?"

Her voice, soft and silky, sent shivers down his spine. "Nothing's wrong."

"Come on, Clint." She put her feet on the seat and hugged her knees. "This is me, remember? You know all my problems. Why don't you tell me yours? We're supposed to be friends, remember?''

''Is that what you want us to be, friends?'' He could have bitten his tongue off the minute the words were out.

Lacey gave him a cautious look. ''Of course.'' She looked out the window a moment, her profile outlined by the moon, then looked back at him. ''Is that what's wrong? You don't want to be friends?''

He ran his fingers through his hair and squeezed his eyes shut, wishing he'd never brought up the subject. Wishing he'd never heard of the word *friendship*.

''Oh,'' she said, her voice sounding . . . hurt. ''I see.''

Damn. ''No, you don't see. You're right, we are friends.'' He slumped down in the seat and dropped his head back. ''Nice night, isn't it?''

''It was.'' Now she sounded angry. ''I think it's ruined now.''

''Sorry.''

''You don't sound like it.''

''I am.'' He straightened and wrapped both arms around the steering wheel, when what he wanted to do was hold her. ''Let's just forget it, all right?''

''No, it's not all right. Either we have a friendship, or we don't. You're either mad at me, or you're not. But I can't read your mind. You're going to have to tell me.''

''I'm not mad at you.'' He sighed. ''And yes, we're friends, if that's what you want.''

''It takes two to make a friendship, Clint. If I want it and you don't, it's not worth much.''

''It's that way with a lot of things in life, isn't it?''

She dropped her knees and faced forward. 'I give up. You're in a bad mood, and obviously enjoying it. If you don't want to tell me what's wrong, I can't help you.''

The toad chorus reached a crescendo, then tapered off for a moment. Into the sudden quiet, Clint said, ''You've got enough on your mind these days. You don't need any more problems to deal with.''

''Thank you so much for doing my thinking for me,

making my decisions for me. Damn it, Clint, I'm a big girl now, in case you hadn't noticed."

The steering wheel dug into his arms. "Oh, I've noticed." Then, because he couldn't help himself, he told her the truth. "You're a big girl, all right. And that," he said, not daring to look at her, "is the gist of my problem."

EIGHT

Lacey pulled her knees up and rested a cheek on them, despair washing over her. "So we're back to that. You don't much like the grown-up Lacey, is that it? You said it before. You don't like what you think I've become."

"No," he claimed fiercely. Clint grabbed her wrist and made her face him. "That's not it, dammit. This has nothing to do with Charles or other men or anything in your past. It has to do with you and me, nothing, no one else."

She felt the seething force of his emotions through his hand on her wrist. It frightened her, thrilled her. Mostly, it confused her because she couldn't tell what emotions drove it. Didn't know what he was talking about. She said as much.

"I'm talking about this."

With a snap of his wrist, she was in his arms. His lips came down on hers, hot, wet, hungry. *Desperate*.

And she was just as desperate. The thought of protest never entered her mind. Somewhere deep inside, this was what she'd been wanting for days, for weeks. His lips on hers, his arms crushing her, his solid chest against her breasts. His labored breathing echoing hers.

She gave, and he gave back. She threaded her fingers through his thick hair, savoring its silkiness. Her heart pounded. Her bones melted. A tiny sound worked its way up her throat.

Clint heard it, and it drove him crazy. Nothing, no one had ever felt so right in his arms as Lacey. Lord, what was he going to do?

He tore his mouth from hers and fought for breath. He pressed her head to his shoulder. It was that, or kiss those honeyed lips again, and he feared if he did, he wouldn't be able to stop.

He wasn't supposed to be doing this. He was supposed to be taking her mind off her problems. But not like this. He'd meant to offer her an hour or two away from the world, where she could relax, take it easy.

"Clint?"

"I'm sorry," he said, his voice not quite steady. "I promised you this wouldn't happen again. I promised you friendship."

He pushed her back then and looked into her eyes, eyes big and wide with confusion. "And I like being friends with you," he said earnestly.

"But?"

"But I keep remembering the taste of your lips, the feel of your hands in my hair—"

Lacey's heart did a little flip-flop in her chest. How could his words affect her as much as his kiss?

"—and I want more."

She swallowed, suddenly nervous. "More?" How could she give more? How could she even think about getting involved with Clint when her life was in such a mess? She pulled from his arms and moved away from him. "How much more?"

He looked at the space of empty seat she'd left between them and sighed. "I guess more than you're interested in giving. More than I have any business asking for."

The river rolled on in the moonlight. The frogs croaked. Lacey stared at Clint across the cab of the pickup. "You want too much."

He stared back. "You want it, too, Lacey."

"No—"

"Don't deny it. When I kiss you, you kiss back."

Panic choked her. "That doesn't mean I want it to go any further."

"No, it doesn't always mean that. But with you it does, unless you're just one terrific little actress."

"Is that what you think?"

"No, it's not what I think," he said harshly. "I think you want the same thing I want."

"Not unless what you want right now is to take me home."

He sat for a moment, his gaze boring into her. With a jerk, he reached for the keys, then stopped. He dropped his hand to his thigh and sat back. "No, that's not what I want. Not when you're mad at me."

Lacey let out a breath. "I'm not mad."

"I know." He angled his shoulders between the seat and the door and leaned back. "You're scared."

She clenched her fists. "What makes you think that?"

"Why else would you deny what your body knows it wants, if not for fear?"

"How about caution, common sense?"

"Where's the common sense in fighting what you feel?"

Through the dust on the windshield, Lacey watched a star blink. "You don't know what I feel."

"Then why don't you tell me?"

She gave a harsh laugh and fought against threatening tears. "I want peace. I want my family and the people I've known all my life to trust me, believe in me, stand by me."

"You're talking about Charles again." He waved the idea away. "I told you I don't care about that."

"Maybe you don't." Her voice cracked. "But you believe it, and that's worse than anything."

"If he lied, then tell me the truth. Give me something else to believe."

"How about believing in *me?*" she cried. "How about

saying you know me better than that, you *know* I wouldn't do the things he accused me of? What have I ever done to make you think I'd do those things?''

He reached for her. She slapped his hand away.

''Ruffles—''

''Don't call me that! The boy who called me that would have stood by me. He wouldn't have believed a man he barely knew over me, no matter who the man was. The Clint Sutherland I remember would have defended me.''

Clint suddenly felt sick to his stomach. She was right. He should have believed in her. He'd known her since the day she was born. She'd never been flighty or disloyal. Honest and true, that had been his Ruffles.

He felt like a fool, and it was a damned uncomfortable feeling. Not totally unfamiliar, he thought with a grimace, but damned uncomfortable.

He had hurt her. Badly. His own unresolved anger with Marianne had made him believe Charles, made him lash out at Lacey.

''I seem to be saying this a lot, but . . . Lacey, I'm sorry.''

She swiped at her eyes with the back of her hand. ''What for this time, Sutherland?''

He forced himself to relax. He'd much rather have her anger than her tears. ''For being my usual jackass self. You're right. I do know you better than that.''

Lacey caught her breath. She wouldn't let herself hope, wouldn't let herself hear things he hadn't said. She'd make him spell it out. ''What do you mean?''

He shifted again, the seat creaking beneath his weight. ''That I was wrong to listen to Charles. I should have believed in you. I *do* believe in you. Charles lied, I see that now. I don't understand why, but I know you didn't run around on him. You wouldn't do that. I just . . .''

The humid breeze brought the scent of sand plums in

bloom. Lacey inhaled the sweet, sweet fragrance. "You just?"

"I think I saw myself in what Charles told me that day. It was like learning the truth about Marianne all over again. Old wounds opened up. I felt all that . . . pain, that betrayal, all over again. And just like the first time, there was no Marianne around to take it out on. When you came home . . . I took it out on you."

The bizarre thought running through Lacey's head made her ill. "I was a substitute."

"I guess."

"And am I still a substitute?"

"What do you mean?"

"Do you still associate me in your mind with Marianne? Is that why you say you want me? Is it her you want, but since she's not here, I'll do? Is that it?"

"Good God, no!" He grabbed her by the shoulders. "I relived the pain, yes, and the anger. But not the wanting, Lacey, never that. When I look at you, I see *you*, want *you*. I've never wanted another woman the way I do you."

"Oh, Clint." Heaven help her, she believed him. It was there in his eyes, in the anguished twist of those beautiful lips, in the bruising strength of his hands on her shoulders. She should have been elated. She wasn't. "That kind of wanting scares me, Clint."

"No, Lacey, no." His grip relaxed, and he pulled her to his chest, where he wrapped his arms around her. "Don't be afraid of me, please. I know I've hurt you a dozen other ways, but I'd never hurt you that way."

She felt his lips against the top of her head, his hands against her back. He did no more than hold her and stroke her. Gradually, she relaxed against him.

"I sure managed to screw this night up."

She couldn't argue with him there. She felt like she'd been put through the wringer on her grandmother's old washing machine.

"I meant to bring you out here for a little peace and

quiet after the hustle of the café. Give you a nice quiet hour or two when you didn't have to think or worry. Just friendly talk to take your mind off your parents.''

She chuckled in spite of herself. ''You sure did that, all right.''

''Did what?''

She straightened away and gave him half a smile. ''Took my mind off my parents.''

''Think they're in bed by now? You ready to go home?''

''Yeah,'' she said leaning back in the seat. She felt drained. ''I guess it's time to go home.''

Fifteen minutes later Clint parked the pickup in his driveway and walked Lacey across the yard to her front door. She reached for the handle on the screen. He stopped her. ''Ruffles—''

''I told you not to call me that.''

He sighed and pulled her into his arms. With his cheek resting on the top of her head, he said, ''When I call you that, it doesn't mean I think you're still a kid. It's a term of affection.''

''Oh.''

''So how long am I going to be in the doghouse over the mess I've made of tonight?''

''That depends.'' She pulled back and looked up at him with eyes narrowed in mock threat. ''Will we ever have to go through any of this again?''

She couldn't see him clearly on the dark porch, but she knew the instant his gaze left her eyes and trailed to her lips. She felt the change, too, in the way his body tensed, the way his breathing changed.

''Parts of it, definitely.''

She never knew what made her ask, but the question, ''What parts?'' came from her mouth in a breathy whisper.

''For starters,'' he pulled her close again, ''this part.''

His kiss was fiercely gentle, hot and searching. Devastating. And over with entirely too soon.

" 'Night, Ruffles.''

He left her standing on the porch while he whistled all the way home. When she turned to let herself in, the key shook in her hand.

When she woke the next morning, the first thing Lacey remembered was Clint's good-night kiss. Its gentleness, its fierceness. Its promise. And her own response. Altogether, the entire subject unnerved her. She sat up in bed.

The ink had barely dried on her divorce papers, and her relationship with her parents was at an all-time low. Her plans for college could be destroyed in an instant if any unexpected expenses popped up. Her entire life was a mess. She had no business getting involved with Clint or any other man. Not until she got her life on track and could stand on her own two feet.

She wanted Clint's friendship. Needed it. But he, it seemed, wanted more. And heaven help her, if he kept kissing her the way he did last night, she'd give him anything he asked for.

Stunned at the admission, Lacey sank back against the pillows. That she could have such blatantly sexual thoughts and feelings frightened her. If Clint could read her mind, there would be no stopping him.

The thought of his hands on her skin made her heart pound. The memory of his arms and his lips left her weak. No, it wouldn't take much persuasion on his part. If he had tried last night, she knew she could easily have ended up lying beneath him in the pickup, giving him everything he wanted. And heaven help her, thanking him for the chance!

And then what? Would they carry on some tawdry, secret affair? One where they had to sneak around late at night to see each other?

My Aunt Fanny.

Lacey knew she could never live that way. She wasn't

the tawdry, secret affair type. The very idea made her sick to her stomach.

She kicked back the covers and crawled out of bed.

There simply would not be anything more between her and Clint beyond what they already had. There couldn't be. Which meant she had better learn to deal with her hormones, or whatever it was that set loose such fierce wanting inside her when he kissed her.

Better yet, she should simply stop kissing him.

While the thought of going beyond kissing scared her, the idea of never tasting his lips again was depressing. How could she stand it?

One day at a time, Lacey, just take it one day at a time.

She showered and dressed, then went to the kitchen. Her mother came in while Lacey was pouring herself a cup of coffee. Tension stiffened Lacey's shoulders. "Morning, Mama. Where's Daddy?"

Irma picked up a paring knife and busied herself peeling an apple. "Where he is every morning by eight o'clock—up at the café, catching up on all the local gossip."

With a flash of Irma's blade, the entire apple peel dropped into a bowl in one long spiral. Lacey shook her head in admiration. She'd never developed that particular skill.

Irma took the basket of apples and a bowl to catch the peels and sat at the table. As she started on another apple, Lacey sat opposite her and watched, remembering all the times she'd sat in just this spot and waited to see if her mother could peel them all without messing up. The tension in her shoulders eased.

"You'd think after working all his life, when he finally retired your father would learn how to relax and enjoy himself. But no, he's got to get down to that café every morning, afraid he might miss something. It's the same way when we're on vacation. I swear, the man never sits still."

Lacey smiled. "Looks like maybe it runs in the family.

I don't see you sitting still. Eight o'clock in the morning, and you're already starting on tonight's dessert.''

Irma kept her gaze on the work in her hands. "Guess maybe you inherited some of that restlessness yourself.''

Lacey stiffened. She wanted to ignore the statement, but made herself ask, "Meaning?''

Irma kept on slipping the knife beneath the apple skin. "Oh, I'm not talking about your divorce, although restlessness might explain it. No, I'm talking about last night.''

"What about last night?''

"It's just a wonder that the first job you've had in years is one where you stand on your feet for hours. Must be exhausting. But when you get off, do you come home to relax? No, not you.''

Lacey bit the inside of her jaw to keep from pointing out that the atmosphere at home was anything but relaxed these days.

"You go out God knows where,'' Irma went on, " 'til all hours of the night with a man who should know better than to run around with a woman who can't help but remind him of his ex-wife.''

"Mama!''

"And then you put on that shameless act right out there on the front porch for the whole neighborhood to see. Honestly, Lacey, I don't know where we went wrong raising you.''

"For crying out loud, Mama, it was barely midnight, and all we did was kiss good night. What were you doing? Peeking out through the curtains?''

Irma's mouth tightened and a flush stole up her cheeks. "Mind your tongue, girl.''

"I'm not a girl anymore, Mama, I'm a grown woman.''

"You're acting like a shameless hussy.''

Lacey felt her nails digging into her palms.

"Clint's a nice man,'' Irma said calmly, her blush receding, "but he's lonely. There aren't all that many available women in a town this size. He needs a good woman who'll stick by him, give him kids to raise. He doesn't need someone who runs with every man that comes along.''

"Clint doesn't think that of me." Lacey pushed her chair back and stood up, her appetite for breakfast long gone. "He knows me better than that. Apparently better than you do."

Irma acted like Lacey had never spoken. "He's the mayor of this town, don't forget. Small town like this, gossip gets around. If you don't care about your reputation, you'd better think about his.''

Lacey carried her coffee cup to the sink and rinsed it. After placing it in the dishwasher with unnecessary violence, she left by the back door. With nothing else to do, she ended up venting her frustration on the weeds in the flower beds around the house.

As a relief valve, weeding didn't help much. She ended up going to work an hour early, just to get away from the house. And her mother. She worried about running into her father at the café, but he had already left there by the time she arrived.

Working kept her mind occupied and let her forget the problem with her mother. She didn't even dwell on what to do about Clint, she was so busy.

Then he showed up for dinner. Just watching him walk across the room made her heart pound.

You're in a bad way, Lacey. The day she couldn't even say hello to a lifelong friend without having her voice catch in her throat was a scary thing. And this was that day.

She took his order, and as she came back from delivering it to the kitchen, she watched him walk across the room to the jukebox. Right then, she knew she was in big trouble. Her mind was definitely in the gutter. She couldn't seem to take her eyes off the way his faded jeans pulled tight across his thighs and tush.

"Do I get some of that tea, or are you just gonna hold it for a while?"

Lacey jerked and nearly sloshed tea all over herself. She looked down guiltily at Mrs. Bonner, then glanced away quickly. The woman was *smirking* at her!

"Guess I know where your mind is," Mrs. Bonner said. "Can't say as I blame you, either. If I were about half a century younger . . ."

Lacey swallowed a nervous giggle. "Yes, ma'am." She poured Mrs. Bonner's tea, then went around the room refilling other tea glasses.

As Clint returned to his booth, his first selection on the jukebox started. Lacey was pouring tea into his glass when Conway Twitty started singing about wanting a lover with a slow hand. The pitcher shook. Tea dribbled down the outside of Clint's glass.

"You're making a mess," he said.

With the blatant message of the song echoing through the room, Lacey couldn't, wouldn't, open her mouth. Neither could she look at Clint. She grabbed an extra napkin and cleaned up the tea, then took a step back, intending to flee. Clint caught her hand and held her there. Conway wanted a lover with an easy touch.

"What are you doing this weekend?" Clint asked.

Lacey's throat went dry, and she couldn't answer.

"Mom and Dad asked me to bring you out to dinner Sunday afternoon."

Conway didn't want someone who would rush things.

The pulse in Lacey's wrist pounded beneath Clint's fingers.

"Lacey?" He tugged on her hand.

She jerked and looked at him.

"Dinner? Sunday? My folks?"

"Oh, uh, sure. Why not?"

"Good. We'll need to get there by one, Mom said."

"Okay."

"You all right? You look a little . . . funny."

"I'm fine. I've got to check on some orders." She slipped from his grasp and practically ran toward the kitchen. Damn. Why had she agreed to go with him? It was a mistake. She knew it. She had no business getting in any deeper with Clint. Her life was a big enough mess as it was. She couldn't even begin to imagine what her mother would say when she learned Lacey was going to Clint's parents' for Sunday dinner.

She should have told him no, that she was busy. But he would have known it was a lie, and he would have been hurt. Hurting him was the last thing she wanted to do.

But . . . dinner with his parents? *Not smart, Lacey.*

He wouldn't be able to kiss her in front of his parents. Maybe it would be safe enough, after all.

Yet judging by her body's response to just being near Clint Sutherland, she doubted this Sunday would be as safe as she hoped.

Lacey was at the cash register when Mrs. Bonner came to pay her ticket.

"Smart move," the woman said, "getting him to take you out to his folks'."

Lacey stared at the woman, appalled. "But I didn't . . ."

Her words sputtered to a halt when the old lady shot her a wicked wink, then tucked her cane under her arm and marched out the door. Still stunned, Lacey's gaze caught Clint's across the room. Then *he* winked at her.

With narrowed eyes and a clenched jaw, Lacey stomped over to his table. "Did you tell her about Sunday dinner?"

Clint raised his hands in surrender. "Of course not. I didn't have to tell her anything. You know there's no such thing as a secret in this place. Everybody in the room can hear everybody else."

Lacey flushed. She knew that. Of course she knew that. On her way back to the kitchen, she kept her gaze firmly on the floor. Even then, she could feel the knowing smiles cast her way by other customers.

Well, damn. She had all but made up her mind that she

and Clint should never be any more than friends. But after this, the whole town would have them courting.

What's wrong with that?

Actually, she kind of liked the sound of that old-fashioned word. Courting. It meant romance, excitement. And it led to commitment, permanence.

And that was probably the farthest thing from Clint's mind. It *should* be the farthest thing from hers. She had enough to deal with.

No, he wasn't courting her. He was interested. Attracted. But that was as far as it went, she was sure.

She hoped.

Two days later Clint was again eating dinner at the café when Maggie whirled in from the kitchen, with a box of pink-wrapped cigars in one hand, her other hand on Mort's shoulder. Mort was ginning to beat all get-out.

"Hey, everybody, I'm a new grandpa!"

"And I'm an aunt!"

All twenty-two people in the café cheered, commented, and asked questions. "Boy or girl?"

"The prettiest little girl you ever saw."

"Donna okay?"

"Donna's terrific."

"She finally bingoed."

Mrs. Bonner frowned at that comment. Then she poked her cane toward Maggie. "They picked out a name yet?"

"Too many," Maggie said. "They've got it narrowed down to either Elizabeth or Amanda."

"How's the new daddy holding up?"

Maggie laughed. "Not quite as well as the new mother, but it looks like he's going to make it."

Another round of laughter.

Through it all, the talk, the laughter, the questions, through the congratulations as Mort and Maggie passed out cigars, Clint watched the play of emotions across Lacey's face. For just an instant, such a look of longing had crossed her features, it had twisted something deep in his gut just to see it. Quickly, so quickly he almost missed it, her hand flew to her stomach, fingers spread protectively, longingly.

Then, as though realizing what she was doing, Lacey dropped her hand, smiled brilliantly, and hugged first Mort, then Maggie.

If she was that affected by the news of someone else's new baby, why, after ten years of marriage, did she not have children of her own?

Personal, Sutherland. Entirely too personal. But he wondered.

He was still wondering that night when he walked Lacey home. He couldn't help the question when it came. "So what do you think about Maggie's new niece?"

Lacey hugged herself and smiled wistfully. "I think it's wonderful. I'm green with envy. I always wanted a little girl."

Her candor surprised him. The question he wanted to ask, the one he knew she expected, hung silently between them.

"Any time Charles and I discussed having kids, he always said it wasn't the right time. I guess for us, he was right."

This time Clint couldn't hold back the obvious question. "Do you think kids would have made a difference in the way things turned out between the two of you?"

She shook her head and scuffed her foot along the sidewalk. "I doubt it. Things might have been different, but not better. I would have been happier, but Charles couldn't have handled the upheaval and confusion children bring to your life. Our reasons for divorcing might have been different, but I think the end result would have been the same."

He wasn't going to ask the next question. He swore he wasn't. Then he did. "What were your reasons for divorcing?"

Her shoulders hunched as if he'd struck her.

"Sorry. Forget I asked. It's none of my business."

If he'd meant to get her to say, "No, that's all right, I'll tell you about it," he failed.

"You always wanted children, didn't you?" she asked him.

"That was a long time ago."

"You don't ever plan to remarry and raise a family?"

He shrugged. "I think about it now and then, but it's not something I worry about."

"I remember your mother telling me about that rocking chair in your living room," Lacey said. "She told me how she used to rock you there, how your grandmother rocked your father, how, when it was time, you would rock your own babies there."

They turned the corner onto their street. The night seemed to call for closeness. Clint took Lacey's hand in his. It felt small and soft, made him feel clumsy.

"I used to think how wonderful it must be to have something like that passed down from generation to generation." She smiled up at him, that wistful look of hers bringing an ache to his chest. "To know exactly where you would sit to rock your children when the time came. To know where your children would rock theirs. How I used to envy you that rocking chair."

The sudden, sharp vision that sprang to his mind made him catch his breath. As clear as day, he could see Lacey sitting in that old wooden chair, holding a towheaded baby to her bare breast. His chair. His baby. His woman.

A shudder ran down his spine. He dropped her hand as though it were on fire, and stuffed his hands in his pockets. "After that time you bonked your head, I thought you hated that chair."

She chuckled. It sounded forced. "I was madder than a hornet at you and Howie, but it wasn't the chair's fault. I'm just glad it didn't suffer in the crash."

"I don't think anything could hurt that old chair." *Except emptiness.*

He left Lacey at the foot of her sidewalk. If he walked

her to the door, he knew he would take his hands out of his pockets. He would touch her, hold her, kiss her. But the vision of Lacey in his grandmother's chair left him shaken. He had some heavy thinking to do. So he kept his hands in his pockets and walked away from her.

NINE

From her bedroom at the back of the house, Lacey heard the doorbell. Her heart pounded. Clint was here. She gave herself a last critical look in the mirror. The pink and white gingham sundress matched her nail polish and complimented her skin and hair coloring better than anything she owned. She straightened the spaghetti straps and smoothed her hands down the fitted bodice. She looked good, if she did think so herself. The gathered skirt swayed with every movement, highlighting her long legs and strappy sandals.

Sudden indecision gripped her. After running off at the mouth the other night about babies and the Sutherland family rocker, maybe she should slip into her old jeans for the day. Would Clint get the wrong idea when he saw how she had dressed to visit his parents?

And if he got such an idea, would it really be the wrong *idea?*

Of course it would. She had her entire life to straighten out. She had no business thinking about rockers and babies and a man whose kisses made her want things she couldn't have.

Which was exactly why she should go out there and tell

Clint to send her regrets to his parents, that she couldn't go to dinner with him. That's what she *should* do.

What she *did*, was touch up her lipstick and dab on a bit more cologne.

A knock sounded on her bedroom door, and her mother entered. "You didn't tell me you were going somewhere with Clint."

"I told you not to set a place for me at dinner."

"He usually has dinner with his folks on Sundays. Is that where you're going?"

Lacey sighed and picked up her purse. "Yes, Mama."

"What are you up to, Lacey June?"

"I'm having dinner with old friends, Mama. I don't know what time I'll be home. See you later."

Her mother followed her to the front door. With each step, Lacey could feel her shoulders tightening. *Leave me alone, Mama.*

"Hi." Clint's smile replaced the tension in her muscles with a fluttering in her stomach. Then, right there with both her parents looking on, he ran his gaze slowly up and down every tingling inch of her. His smile widened. "You look great."

Funny how it only then occurred to her that blue was normally a cool color. How then could his blue eyes look so hot?

Behind her, Irma shifted restlessly.

Lacey wanted to tell Clint how good she thought he looked. The crisp, white shirt highlighted his year-round tan. Sharply creased jeans hugged his legs.

"Headin' on out to the farm?"

Lacey jumped at the sound of her father's voice.

"That's right," Clint said. "I guess we'd better get going, or we'll be late. You ready?" he asked Lacey.

Her throat too dry to speak, Lacey nodded. Clint held the door open for her. When she stepped past him, her arm brushed his shirt sleeve. It felt like an electrical shock. Her eyes flew to his. His widened.

"What time will you be back?" Irma wanted to know.

While Lacey stepped onto the porch, Clint turned to her mother. "Don't worry, Mrs. H." Lacey looked in time to see him wink at her mother. "I'll have her home by sunup."

"Clint Sutherland, shame on you!"

"Relax, doll." He leaned over and kissed Irma on the cheek. "I was only teasin'."

But Lacey noticed, if her parents didn't, that Clint never answered Irma's question.

As soon as they backed out of the driveway, Lacey turned on him. "I can't believe you said that to my mother."

Clint merely shrugged. "She was frowning so hard, I couldn't resist teasing her. She didn't seem to take it well. Anything wrong?"

"She thinks I'm bad for your reputation."

"You're kidding."

"I'm not."

With a devilish grin, Clint wiggled his brows and asked, "Do you want to be?"

"Want to be what?"

"Bad for my reputation."

"Forget it, Sutherland."

"I mean, if you do," he said with mock seriousness, "I don't think I'd mind."

"I'll bet."

He pulled the pickup out onto the highway. Something in the bed thumped. Lacey looked through the back window and saw the bed was loaded with fifty-pound bags of cattle feed. "For your dad?" she asked.

"No, actually, it's for his cattle."

Lacey rolled her eyes. "How does he like living out on the farm?"

Clint smiled. "He loves it. When he first took it over after Uncle Lester died, he wasn't sure he could stand giving up the feed store. I don't think he trusted me to run it the way he had for so many years."

"What does he think now?"

"He's decided maybe the kid knows a thing or two. Besides, you couldn't blast him off that farm. Mom, either."

At the intersection a few miles south of town, Clint turned west on Highway Sixty-two. They drove past fields of winter wheat so bright a green it almost hurt her eyes to look, and fields of fresh-plowed Oklahoma red clay.

The sun was shining, the sky was blue, and the world was suddenly wonderful. Lacey took a deep breath, savoring the fragrance of spring. For now she would ignore the clouds on the horizon, both the real ones to the west and the personal ones in her life.

"Nice lipstick," Clint said.

Lacey looked at him out the corner of her eye. "Thanks."

"You got any more of it with you?"

"Of course. I'd be glad to share, but I don't think it's your color."

"I'm sure you're right." He slowed down and pulled the pickup off the highway onto the shoulder.

"What's wrong?"

"Nothing that can't be fixed," he said. He put the pickup in park, then raised a hip and pulled a handkerchief from his back pocket. "Come here." He took her by the arm and started pulling her across the seat.

"What are you doing?"

"What I've been wanting to do from the minute I saw you in this dress."

He used the handkerchief to wipe her lipstick away. Her heart thumped at his touch. An instant later, he replaced the handkerchief with his lips.

Lacey froze. Her mind told her to pull away. Her body wouldn't move. Liquid warmth gushed through every part of her, and she closed her eyes to hold the heady excitement inside.

His lips, warm, moist, and skillful, took her breath away. He took, she gave.

Clint tried, really tried, to keep it light and simple, to

pull away after just a taste. Ah, but what a taste. The sweet raspberry flavor of her lipstick mingled with the honeyed taste of pure Lacey and drew him in like a bee to nectar.

He pushed his fingers along her nape and into her hair, glad, so glad that she'd left it loose and free-flowing. It caressed him, tangled its silken threads around his fingers and anchored him to her. Right where he wanted to be.

The little sound she made in her throat drove him crazy, made his blood rush, his ears roar. He pulled her flush against his chest and groaned. She was so soft, so delicate in his arms.

The roaring in his ears grew louder. A thundering and whistling whooshed around them, and the world rocked.

Lacey popped her eyes open in horror and pushed away. "Clint!"

"Did you feel it?" He rested his forehead against hers, his eyes still closed. "The earth moved, Lacey. Kiss me again." He reached for her with his lips.

She backed away. "No." Her senses were slowly returning. "It was a truck."

With one hand still on the back of her head, he pulled. "If you can't tell the difference between a kiss and a truck, we better try this again."

"No." Even to her, her giggle sounded high and nervous. "I mean, the earth didn't move. A truck made the pickup sway. Clint, we're sitting right on the highway. Everybody driving by can see us."

"Do you care?" He pulled and leaned at the same time, until their lips almost touched.

Her senses were deserting her again. She knew it the minute she whispered, "No."

The second kiss was no less urgent than the first. Teeth and lips and tongues dueled, took and gave. Breaths, fast and heavy, mingled with a moan, a sigh.

When they came up for air, Lacey was appalled to find Clint leaned back toward the door, with herself draped along his body, across his chest, her arms wound around his neck.

"I think," Clint said, his gaze roaming her face, "that we're not going to be 'just friends' much longer."

Fear. Confusion. And yes, excitement. They raced through her.

"You know that, don't you?" he asked, the deep rumble of his voice vibrating in her chest.

Unable to speak, Lacey shook her head.

"Oh yes, you do. You want it as much as I do."

With heart racing, Lacey levered herself up and away from him. Clint rose and came with her, never letting her more than a few inches from him.

"How can you know what I want?" she whispered frantically. Why couldn't she take her eyes from his lips?

"Because you tell me you want me."

She felt breathless, cornered. "I haven't told you anything like that."

"Sure you have." The corners of his lips curved up. He touched his thumb to the hollow of her throat. "This fluttering right here tells me."

The fluttering grew more violent.

"This pounding, too." His hand pressed half of one breast and rested over her heart. "This pounding says a lot."

The weight of his hand, the hard heat of his fingers where they rested on her bare skin just above the straight bodice of her dress, made her tremble, made her want . . .

"And then there's this." He ran the backs of his fingers across the tips of her breasts.

Lacey gasped and cried out. Her nipples hardened instantly; her breasts swelled. She clamped her eyes shut to keep him from seeing what was happening inside her. An empty, hungry throbbing started down below her belly. God, that he could do this to her with just a touch!

His knuckle beneath her chin tilted her head up. "Look at me, Lacey," he whispered over the hum of the engine.

She did. And she regretted it. His eyes pierced her, shot into her soul and read all her secrets, all her longings.

"It's going to happen," he said. "We both know it. And when it does, I think maybe the earth really will move. For both of us."

He traced a finger across her cheek, making her shiver.

"Heaven help me, I've never met a woman like you before. No one has ever responded to me, to my touch the way you do. You turn me on something fierce. This time I can't even blame it on your nail polish."

"Nail . . . polish?"

"When you wear red polish, I go crazy."

"Maybe pink affects you the same way."

"No." His voice vibrated somewhere low in her belly. "This time it's just you that turns me on. All of you."

A few feet outside the pickup, a car zoomed past on the highway. From the phone lines overhead, a meadowlark sang out. The next car, just an instant later, honked at them.

Clint grinned. "I guess we better go, huh?" He took his hands away, and Lacey struggled for breath. "I think I messed up your hair," he said, his grin crooked. "I know I messed up your lipstick."

Lacey swallowed. *You messed up my mind, too, Clint Sutherland.*

He pulled the pickup out onto the highway, and Lacey did her best to straighten her hair. But it was impossible to put on lipstick with her hands shaking so violently. They turned off the highway onto a dirt and gravel section line road that bounced her around the seat and jostled the bags of feed in the bed. She didn't get her lipstick on until Clint stopped the pickup in the shade of the huge old pecan tree at the edge of his parents' yard.

Hoping to avoid Clint's touch, Lacey didn't wait for him to come around and open her door for her. She climbed out of the pickup and met him at the sidewalk. The ploy failed. Clint placed his hand against her lower back and walked beside her.

As she'd feared, the mere touch of his hand sent her heart pounding again, when it had barely settled down. Her cheeks felt hot, her lips puffy. Lord, his parents were going to take one look at her and know what she and Clint had been doing.

Clint opened the back door and led her directly into the kitchen. The aroma of fresh, hot bread went straight to Lacey's empty stomach.

Clint's mother turned from taking a pan of golden brown rolls from the oven. "There you two are," she said, her eyes smiling softly. "We were beginning to worry about you."

Lacey felt a guilty flush creep up her neck and over her cheeks.

Mrs. Sutherland set the pan of rolls next to the stove and took off her oven mitt. She came and gave Clint a big hug and kiss, then did the same with Lacey.

Nostalgia swamped Lacey. How many times in years past had this elegant, lovely woman hugged her? She had always remembered Joyce Sutherland as the lady with the soft eyes and cupid's mouth. Her yellow-gold hair was always in place, yet she never seemed to fuss over it. Never seemed to fuss over anything personal, except her family.

Joyce held her at arm's length. "Goodness, it's been simply forever, Lacey. Let me look at you." As she searched Lacey's face, Joyce's eyes widened.

Lacey panicked, the urge to bolt coming on strong. She knew! Joyce Sutherland knew what Lacey and Clint had been doing in the pickup on the way here! Lacey read it in the woman's eyes.

Joyce glanced briefly at Clint with a raised brow, then gave Lacey a brilliant smile. "My, what a lovely woman you've grown into."

"I'll second that."

At the intrusion of the male voice, one not gravelly enough to belong to Clint's father, the three in the kitchen turned toward the dining room.

Lacey felt the bold stare from the man's deep brown eyes right down to her skin. There was something familiar about him. He stood maybe an inch taller than Clint's six feet, with hair so black, it gleamed midnight blue where the light struck it. Knock-out handsome, with a cocksure grin on his face. His left arm was bound in a white cast and held before him in a sling.

"Lacey," Joyce said, "you remember Clint's cousin, Alex, don't you? My sister Betty's boy, from Meeker?"

At the sound of his name, Lacey recognized him. "Of course," she said smiling at him. "Cousin Alex of the matching belt buckles."

Alex cocked his head in question.

"The National High School Finals Rodeo," she offered. "You and Clint took first in Team Roping?"

Alex chuckled. "That was so many rodeos ago, I'd almost forgotten."

"Too many rodeos ago," Joyce said. She shook her finger at Alex. "Just look at what you've done to yourself this time. Rodeoing's a fool thing to do. You ought to give it up."

"It's only a busted arm, Aunt Joyce."

"Only? What's next, a broken head? That's about the only thing you haven't had in a cast yet, but I think maybe you've landed on it a few too many times."

"Aw, come on. Clint used to rodeo. I don't remember you giving him such a hard time about it."

"Clint grew up, dear." Joyce stood on tiptoes and kissed his cheek to soften her words. "You never did."

Clint's father came in the back door. He greeted Lacey with affection, his laughing eyes warming her, his smile contagious. She relaxed for the first time since Clint had picked her up.

"How long before dinner?" he asked Joyce. "Clint's brought me a load of feed we need to get down to the barn. Looks like it might rain before the day's over."

"The rain, and the feed, will just have to wait," Joyce told him. "I'm putting dinner on the table now."

Fred Sutherland looked out the window over the sink and searched the sky.

"Forget it, Dad." Clint grinned. "You know it won't dare rain without Mother's permission."

Clint's prediction turned out to be true. Clouds rolled in and blocked the sun during dinner, but the rain held off.

While they ate, Clint's father mentioned a trip he and Joyce were planning in a couple of weeks.

"What about the farm?" Clint asked.

"Neighbor down the road, McConnell, you know him. He's got a boy who's going to come over every morning. I was wondering if you'd have time to come by at night."

Clint agreed, and Fred told him what all would need to be done.

After the meal, all five of them groaned their way through Joyce's pecan pie still warm from the oven.

While Lacey helped Joyce clear the table, Clint's father said, "Come on, son, let's get that feed into the barn before your mother forgets to keep the rain on hold."

Clint hesitated. He didn't much care for the way Alex's eyes followed Lacey's every move all afternoon. "Let's give it a few minutes, Dad, so Lacey can go with us."

Alex rose from the table, his gaze taunting. "You don't really want to make a pretty little thing like her traipse through barnyard manure in those dainty white sandals, do you?"

Clint glanced at Lacey's feet. Damn, Alex was right.

Lacey gave Clint a rueful grin. "I'm sorry. I guess I'm really not dressed for it."

Alex sauntered up next to her and put his hand on her bare shoulder. Clint stiffened. He and Alex had always been close friends. Blood ran thick in their families. But right that minute, Clint had the strongest urge to break Alex's one good arm. At the very least, the hand that was touching Lacey's bare skin.

"Now look what you've done," Alex said. Then he leaned down to Lacey, his voice turning intimate. "What do you want to trouble yourself with a man like him for? Never apologize for looking pretty, honey."

Honey? He called her honey? Clint felt his blood boil. "You're right," he said. "Lacey's not dressed for it. But you are."

Clint clamped a hand around his cousin's neck, wishing it was two hands, and wanting desperately to squeeze. Hard.

"Hey, I've got a broken arm. I won't be any help."

"You can supervise," Clint said tightly.

Lacey watched Clint drag a protesting Alex out through the back door. Behind her, Joyce chuckled.

"My, my," the woman said. "I don't remember the last time Clint was jealous over a woman."

Lacey whirled and gaped. "No, surely—"

"Yes. Surely." Joyce smiled warmly. "Personally, I think it's wonderful."

TEN

By the time Clint and Lacey left for home, the wind whipped fiercely at everything in its path. Thick black clouds rolled across the sky, flinging fat, cold raindrops before the north wind.

Clint took the three-mile stretch of dirt road as fast as its rough surface allowed, knowing how slippery the red clay got during a heavy rain. He didn't slow down until he hit pavement.

The sky opened. It was like having someone turn over a barrel of water just above the windshield. Solid sheets of rain poured across them, and the wind rocked the pickup like it was a toy. Clint slowed to a crawl. The wipers slapped noisily back and forth. He took his eyes off the road long enough to glance at Lacey, and saw her shiver. "Cold?"

"Freezing," she said.

Clint patted the seat beside him. "Come here and get warm. I'll turn the heat on."

She scooted over next to him, and he put his arm around her. The skin of her bare shoulder felt like ice. "You *are* cold."

When she nodded, her teeth chattered. "If I'd known it was going to do this, I'd have dressed warmer."

"That's all right." He grinned. "I don't mind warming you up." He rubbed his hand up and down her arm and felt her goose bumps fade, her shivers ease.

Even the rain let up to a mere downpour.

Lacey let Clint's heat seep into her and began to relax. She should move back across the seat. She knew she should. But she didn't. The spot at his side felt as if it were made to accommodate her.

"Thanks for bringing me along today," she said. "Your parents are just the way I remembered them. I enjoyed myself."

The hand on her upper arm tightened. "Even with Alex?"

She fought a smile. So, his mother had been right. "Alex is a rascal."

The fingers tightened again. "I didn't like him touching you."

She grinned then. "He's harmless."

"Huh. That man has been under more skirts than I can count. If he'd had you alone for two minutes, he'd have been under yours, too."

Lacey leaned away, looked at him, and scowled. She removed his arm from behind her shoulders and dropped it across his lap, where he let it fall. "I believe I've just been insulted."

Clint looked away from the rain-slick road long enough to show his surprise. The hand she'd just dropped in his lap had already moved to her knee. She tried to push it away, but he held on.

"I wasn't insulting you," he protested. "Actually, it was more of a compliment. Alex has very discriminating taste."

"So," she said slowly, "do I. He wouldn't get 'under my skirt' as you put it, because I wouldn't let him."

He grinned. "Good. Glad to hear it."

She would have told him then and there that *he* would never get under her skirt, either. The only problem was, under her skirt was exactly where his hand was at that moment. His hand disappeared beneath pink gingham and rested just above her right knee. She would have moved away, but the little circle he was drawing with his thumb on the inside of her leg paralyzed her. If she moved away, he'd have to stop. And heaven help her, she didn't want him to stop.

Lacey, Lacey, you're asking for trouble.

"Firm."

"What?" she asked.

Clint's Adam's apple bobbed with a swallow. "Your thigh. It's firm." He swallowed again. "And silky. I've been . . . wondering."

Now she swallowed. Hard. "Maybe . . ." *Go on, stupid, say it.* "Maybe you should take your hand away."

He negotiated a curve and, without taking his eyes off the road, asked, "Do you want me to?"

The roughness of his voice made her breasts tighten.

Say yes! Tell him to take his hand away. Move over so he can't reach you.

"Lacey?"

She closed her eyes and whispered, "No."

His hand, and the rest of him, stilled. Then that teasing thumb moved again, circling, circling across the sensitive skin of her inner thigh. Moving higher.

Outside, the rain fell heavier again. Lacey didn't care. The world could flood, as long as Clint didn't take his hand away.

By the time they pulled into her driveway, it was dark, and the full-fledged deluge was back. When Clint stopped the pickup, Lacey knew the garage was no farther away than five feet, but she couldn't see it. And Clint's hand now rested midway up her left thigh beneath her dress. His little finger moved restlessly, closer and closer to the part of her that throbbed heavily with every breath she took.

Stop it, Lacey. Stop him. Stop while you still can.

"I have to go." She started across the seat, then cried out and froze. Her movement had forced the most intimate part of her body against the edge of his hand. She couldn't look at him, for she knew he felt her heat, her wanting.

And he did. He felt them clear through to his soul. And he felt what the knowing did to his body.

He knew he should let her go. She would get drenched, maybe catch cold. But if he didn't let her go . . .

No, he couldn't do what he wanted to do. He *had* to let her go. He just didn't know if he was strong enough. A moment later, he found out he wasn't.

He slammed off the headlights and killed the engine. With a low growl, maybe of protest at his own actions, maybe of surrender to the lure of the moist heat against his hand, he started toward her.

Whatever demon had held Lacey motionless and locked her breath in her throat finally cut loose. She met Clint halfway and fell against him.

"Lacey," he murmured against her lips. "Lacey."

Lips and breath, arms and legs, all entangled each other. There was no telling where one person started and the other stopped. It was a kiss, but it involved both their entire bodies, from head to toe. And it was frantic, as if neither could get enough of the other.

Yes! her heart cried. She wanted this, needed him. His hands were everywhere, and so were hers, clutching him, desperate to touch, to feel. The sudden image of the red foil pouch she'd seen in his wallet teased her, scorched her. Did he still carry it?

The snaps on his Western shirt gave with only a slight tug, and she was touching hard, hair-roughened chest. Lord, the feel of him.

When she touched his bare skin, Clint shuddered. He reached beneath her skirt again and filled his hand with a firm, silk-clad cheek.

She spread kisses down his jaw, along his throat, and onto his chest. Another shudder ripped through him. He pulled her flush against him. "Feel that," he said, thrusting his hips against her. "Feel what you do to me."

She gasped. "We have to stop." Her breath rasped in

her throat. "We can't do this, Clint. Not in my parents' driveway. Not . . ."

He held her even tighter, his chest heaving. "I know. Not like this, I know." With more willpower than he knew he had, he pulled away and gripped her shoulders. In the storm-darkened twilight, her eyes, her lips wet from his, gleamed.

"But when we do," he said, a slow grin spreading, "it's going to be explosive. Sheer dynamite, Ruffles."

Lacey pulled out of his grasp and dropped her head back against the seat, shaken and stunned by what had nearly just happened. "We can't do this, Clint. *I* can't do this."

"We're not doing anything. This time," he said.

"There won't be a next time."

"Why not?"

Was that anger, or hurt in his voice? "Because that's the way I want it," she said firmly.

"The hell it is. You were so hot for me a minute ago I probably have blisters on my hand."

"Don't be crude."

"Don't lie to me. Or are you lying to yourself?"

"I don't go in for casual sex."

"Casual!" he shouted. "There's not a damn thing casual about what we feel for each other, and you know it. You're scared."

"Yes."

"Of me?" he cried.

Tears welled in her eyes. God, she was so confused. She was hurting him, hurting herself. But she didn't know what to do, dammit. "No, not of you. Of this . . . this whatever it is between us. It's so . . . so . . ."

"I think the word you're looking for is 'powerful.' "

She swallowed. "Maybe."

"And it will be, Lacey. When we make love—"

"Make love? Is that how you see it?"

"Don't you?"

Lacey sagged against the seat. Why was she arguing

with him, when she didn't even know which side of the argument she was on? She gave a wry chuckle. "If nothing else, I think we'll definitely make fire."

Clint found her hand in the darkness and laced his fingers through hers. She hadn't said "we would," she'd said "we will."

"Can we just . . . take things a little slower?" she asked.

His heart thundered louder than the storm. He laughed with relief. Slower. He could deal with that. He hoped. He squeezed her fingers gently. "Any way you want it, Ruffles. You want slower, we'll go slower. For as long as we can stand it."

Lacey's nerves leaped in response. She'd all but agreed to make love with him. Was she out of her mind?

Yes!

No. She wasn't. Nothing had ever felt so right in her life as when she and Clint were together.

But if she didn't stop thinking about how "together" they had almost become a few minutes ago, she would end up doing something downright lewd in her own driveway.

"I better go in," she said.

"Give it a minute," he answered. "Rain's starting to let up."

"Then can we talk about something else?" she asked, hoping her voice didn't sound as desperate to him as it did to her.

"Pick a topic."

She thought for a moment, then smiled to herself. "Okay, here's one. Just how, precisely, did you pick the name Ruffles for me?"

He laughed and she felt the tension leave his hand. "Hell, I was only about seven when you were born. Howie was so proud to have a baby sister. I remember your mother kept reminding me that your name was like the lace on those little gowns she used to dress you in. Then your dad would come along and point out that you always wore ruffles, too. What does a seven-year-old boy know about lace and ruffles? I kept getting them mixed up.''

''And after you learned the difference?''

''It was too late. I was used to calling you Ruffles.''

Lacey chuckled.

''Okay, it's my turn now,'' Clint said.

''Have at it.''

Clint took a deep breath hoping he wasn't about to make a big mistake, but knowing he had to ask. ''What happened to you and Charles?''

She tried to jerk her hand from his. He held on. ''Talk to me, Lacey.''

After a long moment, with no sound but the rain hitting the roof, her voice came, sounding tortured. ''I can't.''

Can't. The bastard had hurt her so badly she couldn't even talk about it. Rage like Clint had never known shot through him. He took a slow, deep breath and prayed for calm. ''If it was that bad, why didn't you come home?''

Lacey shook her head. ''I needed some time alone. I wasn't ready to cope with Mama's objections to the divorce.'' She gave a sad laugh. ''If I'd known Charles had been here, that my parents would believe him over me, I might not have come home at all.''

''Don't say that,'' he told her fiercely. The thought of not having her in his life sent a bleakness through him so strong it twisted his gut.

He squeezed her hand. ''Did it help, going off on your own?''

She let out another sad chuckle. ''I thought so at the time. Until my parents came home.''

''You mean until I opened my big mouth and repeated Charles's lies.''

This time it was Lacey who squeezed his fingers. ''You had your reasons for believing him. I understand that.''

The guilt was back, threatening to choke him. ''That's no excuse for—''

''But you don't believe him anymore. That's the difference, Clint. Mama and Daddy still do.''

Clint brought her hand to his mouth. Her skin was smooth and cool against his lips. "They'll come around, you'll see."

He lowered their joined hands to his thigh. "Actually, you probably did the right thing, taking off like you did. When Marianne and I split, I could have used a little time away from well-meaning friends and family."

In the darkness, he saw Lacey turn her face toward him. "Why didn't you take off?"

He shrugged. "No place to go. No place would have been far enough away."

She squeezed his hand again. "I know what you mean. I went to California, and even that wasn't far enough."

"California? What did you do there?"

"Hibernate, mostly."

"Don't you have family out there?"

"A cousin. Her husband's company sent him to London for several months. I house-sat so she could go with him."

They sat in comfortable silence for several minutes, holding hands, watching the rain.

"It's almost stopped," she said, indicating the rain.

It was true. As suddenly as the downpour had started nearly an hour earlier, it had stopped. It was barely sprinkling now. The house was dark, no lights shining.

Clint didn't want to let her go, but knew he had to. "Can I walk you to the door?"

She squeezed his fingers again. "Yes. Please."

Neither hurried through the few remaining raindrops. On the porch, he wrapped his arms around her and closed his lips over hers. Her soft sigh went to his head. And lower.

Then the most incredible thing happened. Something that hadn't happened to him during a good-night kiss in probably twenty years. The porch light came on.

He'd barely registered that intrusion when the damned front door flew open!

Clint and Lacey broke apart and stared at each other for a stunned moment. She looked like a woman who'd just been thoroughly kissed. And she looked embarrassed, guilty. And frightened?

At a loud throat-clearing in the doorway, Clint turned toward Mrs. H. The woman's look would have sent a less assured man scurrying for cover.

"Well, I never," Lacey's mother said. "Out there fogging up the windows all this time, right in plain view of the entire neighborhood. I'd be ashamed."

"Wait—" Clint began.

But Mrs. H. ignored him and looked at Lacey. "Trying for another notch on your bedpost?"

Lacey gasped. Clint was stunned. He couldn't believe her mother would say such a thing.

"And you," she said to him. "Just out for a good time, I suppose, with somebody who's known to be easy?"

Clint's mouth fell open in shock. "I don't believe you said that."

"Irma," Mr. H. said from behind her, "leave the kids alone."

Her husband took her by the hand and led her away from the door.

"They're not kids," Irma protested. "They're adults, and they should have more sense."

Clint was floored. He couldn't believe Mrs. H. acted that way. Rage nearly choked him. He looked at Lacey. "What the hell's gotten into her?"

She looked tired, shaken. She shook her head.

"You don't mean she's like this all the time!"

Her sad little smile was filled with irony. "Only since I showed up."

A memory flashed, of the night he'd told Lacey about Charles' visit, of how he had treated her after that, until he'd come to realize how wrong he'd been.

He knew her parents had believed Charles in the beginning. He just couldn't conceive of Irma Hamilton treating Lacey this way, no matter what she thought. His rage fought with bewilderment. Mrs. H. had been one of the kindest, most loving women he'd ever known. Maybe a little too concerned over the opinions of others, maybe a tad smug now and then that her husband had been—still was—an important man in the community. But even when she and Lacey had been at odds, the Hamiltons had always stood up for each other, presenting a united front to the world.

Lacey interrupted his thoughts with a quiet, "Good night, Clint."

He pulled her to him for one last hug and kissed the top of her head. "I'm sorry, Ruffles."

"Don't be," she said. "It's not your fault."

With a finger beneath her chin, he raised her head until she looked at him. "It's not yours, either."

She said nothing, just gave him that sad little smile again, and went inside.

He cursed all the way home.

ELEVEN

Clint spent a restless night. The scene between Lacey and him in the pickup kept getting all mixed up with her mother's viciousness at the front door.

He wanted Lacey. There was no denying that. He wanted her in his bed, in his life. He wanted to protect her, love her.

Love?

He could, he knew. It would be easy, so easy to let loose of his feelings the way he nearly let loose of his control earlier in the night. She was so warm and giving, so beautiful. And she did things to his body, hot, violent things no woman had ever done before.

But he worried about her. He'd known she would have trouble with her mother, but he hadn't suspected how much. Lacey was hurting, both from whatever had happened with Charles, the man's unconscionable lies, and what looked like total rejection from her own mother.

He wanted to make it all go away so she could laugh and smile again. He wanted to make her happy, see those gray eyes sparkle.

He smirked and untangled the sheet from around his legs.

Sure, he wanted those things for her. But he wanted

them for himself, too. If she was happy, if she didn't have to worry about so many other things, she'd be able to concentrate more on him and what was happening between them.

Selfish, ulterior motives. He knew it, but couldn't seem to stop the wanting.

At least his own parents had been nice to her. True, they didn't know what Charles had told the Hamiltons. It was none of their business. He'd like to think that even if they'd heard the lies, they would have been smarter than he and Lacey's parents had been.

Then there had been Alex. Clint stared at the ceiling and remembered the fury that had swamped him at the sight of his cousin's hand on Lacey's bare shoulder. Lord help him, when was the last time he'd felt even a twinge of jealousy?

Not since Marianne. Even then, not to the point of wanting to strangle someone. With surprising detachment, he wondered if Alex and Marianne had ever . . . No, Alex wouldn't have. Marianne, now, was a different story. Back then the mere possibility would have killed Clint. Now, it didn't seem to matter at all. So long as Alex kept his hands away from Lacey.

Clint didn't know what he could do about the situation with Lacey's mother. Nothing, most likely. Lacey would in all likelihood resent his interference, and her mother wouldn't listen—not if tonight was anything to go by.

He could, of course, back off from Lacey, leave her alone. Give her time to straighten out some of her problems. She had asked if they could slow things down. He could do that for her, give her the space and time she seemed to need.

He could.

During the next few days, Clint tried. He tried to slow things down, to give Lacey the space and time she needed. He really tried. If he tried hard enough, he could do it.

The hell he could. About as easily as he could stop

breathing and still live. He didn't have that kind of willpower.

Lacey.

He wanted her next to him in his big, lonely bed. He wanted her beneath him. He wanted to lose himself inside her, feel her surrounding him with her heat, her passion. He wanted her.

After four days of staying away, he found himself waiting for her outside the café Thursday night, listening to the season's first crickets.

When Lacey stepped out onto the sidewalk, she was obviously surprised to see him. "What are you doing here?" she asked.

He stuffed his hands in his pockets to keep from reaching for her. "Can I walk you home?"

Lacey bit her lip to keep from asking where he'd been, why he'd stayed away. She had learned something about herself during the past four days, about what she wanted in her life, what was important to her.

It had come as somewhat of a shock to realize that things she thought were important, things on which she had been hinging her future, paled in comparison to her feelings for Clint. Her mother could rant at her. Her father could get that hangdog look, sigh and shake his head in disappointment—in both her and her mother. Lacey could even fail to support herself well enough to go back to college.

She could live with all those hurts and disappointments. As long as she could see Clint, be with him, know he cared.

But she didn't know if he cared, not really. He was here, and she knew he wanted her. But he'd stayed away four whole days! She'd feared her mother had run him off for good with her stunt Sunday night. Yet here he was, wanting—*asking*—to walk her home.

She had no idea where a relationship with Clint might lead. She only knew she had to find out. She smiled at him. "I'd like that."

The smile he gave back was tentative. That puzzled her.
They sauntered across the street and down the sidewalk
toward home.

"I've missed you," he admitted.

Lacey felt her heart contract. "I've missed you, too."

They turned the corner onto their street. A dog behind
a house barked twice, then quieted. Somewhere out on
Main an engine revved.

"You said you wanted things to slow down," he told
her.

"Yes, I said that, didn't I?"

"You sound . . ."

"Like I wished I hadn't said it," she finished for him.
Heavens, where had her nerve come from?

Clint stopped and pulled his hands from his pockets,
slowly. His eyes were in shadow, but she felt them on
her face like a soft caress. His voice, when it finally came,
was hoarse with emotion. "I want you, Lacey."

She hadn't realized how those words affected her until
she heard the whimper from her own throat. "Don't say
that," she whispered harshly. "Not here, not now, when
we can't . . ."

She couldn't finish, didn't need to. Clint didn't need to
hear the rest. What she'd already said was more than
enough to send his heart soaring, his pulse pounding.

"Come here," he whispered. He took her by the hand
and pulled her behind Mrs. Samuels's twenty-year-old
lilac bush. "I'll be damned if I'll give your mother
another shot at either of us. But if I don't get to hold
you, kiss—"

She flew into his arms. "Oh, Clint."

Sweet. So damned sweet to feel her arms around his
neck, her slender body pressed against him. She took his
breath away. Then, with his lips and teeth and tongue, he
vowed to do the same to her.

The air smelled of lilacs. Lacey smelled of woman.
Warm, giving, vibrant woman.

It was the piercing heat in his loins several minutes later

that made him pull back, chest heaving, hands shaking. Lacey had been right. Not here, not now, when they couldn't. He held her, and she clung to him and sighed. Her hair slid like silk through his fingers.

He didn't know when they would get the chance to be alone and finish what they started every time they touched. But soon. It had to be soon.

After several long minutes, their breathing calmed, the tension eased. "Ready to go?" he asked.

"No." She pulled away and smiled. "But we'd better, or hiding behind this bush will have been for nothing."

He answered her smile. If that was a joke about her mother, then the situation must be getting better. She was handling it.

He stole a quick kiss, then let her go. At the foot of her sidewalk, they stopped. "Walk you home tomorrow night?" he asked.

She took a backward step up her sidewalk and grinned. "Only if you promise we won't end up *underneath* that lilac bush."

He would have laughed at her teasing, but he couldn't. The sharp, erotic images her words summoned nearly buckled his knees. Black sky, moist earth, the smell of lilacs. And Lacey, with her delicate arms and long legs wrapped around him. . . .

He took a deep breath and choked on it.

Lacey laughed and took another step back. "What? No promise?"

He looked at her with growing amazement. She'd done it on purpose! She had deliberately chosen those words to arouse him. This was an entirely new Lacey. Or maybe the old one, for all he knew, getting her confidence back. Whatever was going on in that mind of hers, he liked it. He grinned at her. "You'll pay for that, woman."

"Oooo. Is that a threat?"

Why, the little devil. "Not on your life, Ruffles. It's a promise."

Her breasts lifted on a sharp intake of breath, teasing

him, taunting him. Then came the slowest, sexiest smile he'd ever seen in his life. Fire shot through his gut.

"Good," she answered. "I'll hold you to it."

During the rest of the week they found no time to be alone except for their short walks at night. An unspoken agreement stood between them, one that stipulated Lacey would not set foot inside Clint's house. If she did, they both knew what would happen once they had the privacy they craved. While they wished for time alone together, neither wanted the distraction of knowing Irma Hamilton would likely bang on the door at *the* most inappropriate moment.

So they waited.

Each night, the walk home seemed shorter. Their kisses turned hungrier, more desperate. And afterwards, when Lacey left him and went to bed, her dreams grew . . . *hotter*.

Saturday saw the annual community Spring Dance. As mayor, Clint was expected to attend. Irma and Neal Hamilton were regulars, Irma bringing her usual lemonade punch for the occasion.

Lacey couldn't bring herself to go to the dance when she got off work. Her mother was too unpredictable these days. If Lacey got near enough to Clint, or any other man, for that matter, to dance, Irma would start in on her again.

Things had been relatively peaceful at home the past week. Her mother had seemed more like her old self again, even teasing Lacey once about sleeping late. Much as she wanted to see Clint, being with him in public, with dozens of people around, was not worth anther blow-up from her mother. Not that Lacey wouldn't be proud to be seen with Clint. It just wasn't the right time. She had to find a way to get through to her mother first.

As excuses went, her mother's attitude was a good one. But Lacey had to admit the truth to herself. She didn't trust herself to be with Clint in public. And if the way he'd held her last night behind the lilac bush was any

indication, she didn't trust him, either. The wanting, the
fierce, hungry ache, was getting out of control. She simply
couldn't bring herself to press her body to his and sway
to seductive music while dozens of people looked on. If
she and Clint didn't both go up in a puff of smoky frustration, they ran the risk of ending up in jail for public
indecency.

So Lacey didn't go to the dance. After work, she
walked herself home, the strains of the live country band
following her down Main Street from the VFW Hall in
the middle of town. One house short of home, she paused
at the lilac bush. The sweet fragrance filled her with a
nearly unbearable ache and evoked the hot desperation she
and Clint had shared in the shadows.

"This is ridiculous," she said to herself. "I'm a grown
woman, twenty-nine years old, and I'm stealing kisses
behind bushes so my mother won't find out."

A dog across the street barked, reminding her she stood
alone, on a dark sidewalk, talking to herself. She took
herself home and went to bed. One night without seeing
Clint, and she was miserable. *You've got it bad, girl.* She
hoped Clint would call tomorrow, that he could find a way
for them to be together.

He did call Sunday, but not until eight o'clock, and not
from his home. He was at the farm, helping his dad catch
up on work so the Sutherlands could leave the next day
as planned, and not leave anything but basic chores for
Clint and the neighbor to do while they were gone.

"I'm sorry," he told her on the phone. "I wanted to
see you today. I wanted to see you last night."

"Me, too," she said. He knew why she'd skipped the
dance because she had told him. "You sound tired."

His sigh made her weak. "I think I am. I've accused
Dad of saving up every backbreaking chore until today,
so I'd have to help him."

"You'll be going out there after work tomorrow?"

"Yeah."

"Will you stop by the café for dinner?"

"I don't know. But if I don't, I'll see you when you get off."

"Promise?"

"You know I can't stay away."

The huskiness in his voice nearly stole her breath. When she didn't say anything, he said, "Lacey?"

She cleared her throat. "I'm here."

"I'll see you tomorrow night."

"All right."

"Sweet dreams. Good night."

The phone trembled in her hand when she hung it up. Sweet dreams? No chance. Hot dreams. Hungry dreams. The same dreams that had plagued her, tormented her ever since the night they came home from the farm. The night the rain trapped them in the pickup. Erotic dreams.

How had it happened? How had she become obsessed with a man's body, a man's touch, a man's smile?

Years ago, she had loved Charles. *Loved* him. Or loved the man she had thought he was. But she didn't remember ever feeling desperate for the mere sight of him. She didn't remember craving the fierce rush brought on by just thinking his name. She didn't remember aching with want day after day.

It was Clint. He drew her to him like Bogart drew Bacall. She chuckled and groaned. In her case, as wild as the urges were that swamped her, maybe it was more like Tarzan drawing Jane.

If Lacey didn't get to see Clint soon, she might very well end up yodeling from the nearest tree in sheer frustration.

When he didn't make it into the café for dinner Monday night, she told herself she would live. He would surely come to walk her home.

And he did.

His smile of greeting looked brittle and faded quickly. Tension radiated from him. The skin over his cheek bones was stretched taut, his shoulders were bunched and quivering. His hands, rammed into his front jeans pockets, were balled into fists. And his mouth, that beautiful mouth that drove her wild, was held firm in grim lines.

"What's wrong?" she asked.

He shivered. The air was warm and balmy, and he shivered.

"Clint?" She put a hand on his arm. It was rock hard. A tremor raced beneath her fingers.

He took a deep breath, then let it out with a crooked smile. "Just tired, that's all."

She could see it now, the lines of exhaustion around his eyes and beside his mouth. She wanted to hold him, press his head to her breast and watch over him while he slept. Wanted to give him ease and comfort. Wanted it desperately. For him. And even more for herself.

But there was more in his eyes than exhaustion. There was heat. Fever. The same heat and fever she had seen in her own eyes in the mirror Sunday night after his phone call. After he'd wished her sweet dreams.

Without her realizing it, her hand trailed up his arm and caressed his cheek. Clint took her hand in his and gripped it tightly

"Let's go," she whispered.

They walked side by side toward home. Clint held on to her hand for dear life. With her touch, he could feel the tiredness slip away, only to be replaced by a new, dangerous energy that drew his nerves taut and made his muscles quiver.

With effort, he relaxed his fingers around hers. He thought maybe thirty-six was too young for a man to suffer from the middle-aged crazies, but he didn't know what else to blame for what he was feeling these days. He'd never been a slave to his emotions before, nor to his hormones. Not, that is, until Lacey came back to town.

He was so deep in thought he hadn't realized they'd reached the lilac bush until Lacey stopped. He looked at her, her face pale and glowing in the moonlight. She squeezed his fingers and smiled.

Clint hesitated. "Lacey . . ."

"What is it?"

"I—" He broke off with a harsh laugh. "The way I feel right now, if I kiss you, we might really end up underneath that damned bush."

Her smile died, her eyes darkened. "Believe me, I know the feeling."

Heat knifed through his belly. "You shouldn't have said that." He tugged on her hand and pulled her behind the bush.

It was a wonder the lilacs didn't go up in flames from the fire that flared when Lacey met his lips with hers. Only the need for breath tore them apart.

With his lower body pressed against hers, Clint held her and fought for control.

"This is stupid," she said against his chest. "Two grown people making out in the bushes. Take me home with you, Clint."

His heart flipped. Blood rushed, and the tightness in his loins turned to a definite hardness. "What will your folks say when you don't come home in time?"

"I don't care." Her fingers dug into his back. "I don't care anymore what they think."

Sanity crowded in. Clint dropped his chin to the top of her head. "But I do, Ruffles. And you do, too, really. Besides," he added, "when it happens for us, I don't want to be rushed. I don't want you to have to hurry home, worrying all the time about facing down your mother. I want you to myself for hours, days."

Lacey shivered in his arms. "Then what are we going to do?"

Lord, how could she talk like this when he was so near to bursting? She was telling him in no uncertain terms that she wanted him as much as he wanted her. It was like putting a match to gasoline. He tipped her head up and took her mouth with his, showing her how he felt.

"I don't know," he said against her lips. "I'll think of something." He nibbled his way to her ear. "I'll find a way, I promise."

"Soon?"

He shuddered. "Keep talking like that, and we'll end up on the ground yet."

She nipped at his ear lobe. "You didn't answer my question."

"Yes, soon." God, what was she doing to his ear? Her teeth, her breath, her tongue . . . He groaned. "Soon, I swear it."

By silent agreement, they stopped kissing, stopped teasing. They leaned against each other and held on until they calmed.

After several quiet moments, Lacey leaned back in his arms with a smile. "Besides," she said. "You promised we wouldn't end up under the bush."

"Oh, no, I didn't," he answered. "That was your idea. I only promised to get even with you for teasing me that night."

With her arm around his waist and his around her shoulders, they walked to the foot of her sidewalk, then parted. Clint stood still and watched her let herself into the house.

She was right about one thing. They couldn't go on this way much longer. He was wound so tight he was afraid he'd snap. And when they kissed, she felt the same way in his arms.

The next night, Lacey caught herself pouting because Clint had to play mayor and wasn't free to walk her home and kiss her good night. She was becoming thoroughly disgusted with herself, with her obsession with Clint.

But even admitting that, she couldn't stop the wanting. When he called Wednesday, she breathed a prayer of thanks that her parents had gone shopping, allowing her to talk without eavesdroppers.

"Isn't this your day off?" Clint asked.

"Yes."

"You want to ride out to the farm with me tonight? We can stop at Jacktown on the way and pick up something for supper. After I take care of the cattle, you can help me round up Mom's attack hens.''

"Her what?''

"Her laying hens. They love her, but they hate my guts. I've got peck holes in my shins. When we're finished we could . . . go to a movie . . . or, uh, not.''

Lacey caught her breath. This was it, then. "What are you asking me, Clint?''

His voice lowered. "I'm not asking, Lacey. I'm answering the question you asked the other night. Remember?''

How could she forget? She still couldn't believe she'd asked him, *What are we going to do?*

And now he was answering.

"Have you changed your mind?'' he asked quietly.

"No,'' she said in a rush of breath. She closed her eyes and felt her heart hammer against her breastbone. "I haven't changed my mind.''

"Then do you want to go?''

"Yes. I want to.''

She heard him let out a breath. "I'll leave here around five-fifteen, go home, and get cleaned up. Is six o'clock okay?''

Lacey swallowed. It was going to happen. They would go to his parents' farm, and sometime during the evening, they would make love. The terrible waiting would be over. The ache deep inside her would ease. She'd be able to hold him, kiss him, touch him. And he would do the same to her. She closed her eyes and swallowed. "Yes. Six.''

"I'll see you then.''

"Uh, Clint?'' Oh Lord. How did a woman ask what she needed to ask? She had never been part of the singles scene.

"Yeah?''

"I'm, uh, not . . . what I mean is, I'm not used to . . .''

"What is it, Ruffles? You can tell me anything, you know that.''

"Fine. All right." She took a deep breath and plunged onward. "How's your wallet?"

"My wallet? You worried I don't have enough money for the movie?"

She heard uncertain laughter in his voice. She opened her eyes and glared at the phone. Was he being deliberately obtuse? "My guess is, we'll never make it to the movie."

A low growl came over the phone. "Do you have any idea what it does to me when you talk like that?"

"But I'm right, aren't I?"

"God, I hope so," he said fervently.

She closed her eyes again. Maybe it would help her to get the words out. "Then we need to talk about . . . what I saw in your wallet a couple of weeks ago."

"I don't know— Oh. Somebody's listening, so you can't talk, right?"

"No, I'm alone. I've just never . . . I never had to . . . Clint, dammit, do you still have that thing in your wallet or not?"

"What thi— Oh, *that* thing." He chuckled. "Of course I still have it. The best I could have used it for these past weeks would have been as a water balloon."

A bark of laughter shot out of Lacey's mouth before she could stop it. "Clint, this is serious."

"I hope so." There was a definite grin in his voice.

"You're making fun of me."

"No way, lady."

"Well, then . . ." She felt her face burn. "Do you think, uh, that is . . ."

"Come on, Lacey," he said, laughing, "spit it out."

She ground her teeth together. "All right, damn you. Is one of those things going to be enough? Oh-God-I-can't-believe-I-said-that."

Another bark of laughter, this time from Clint. She buried her burning face in her hand and groaned, while he kept laughing. Finally, between gusts of laughter, he said, "Lord, Lacey, I love you."

Lacey jerked upright and dropped her hand from her face. He couldn't mean it. He couldn't. Not the way she—

No. He meant it as a friend, that's all. As soon as he said the words, his laughter had stopped. Was he afraid she might take him seriously?

"Lacey?"

"I'm here."

"In answer to your question, no." No laughter in his voice now, only softness and dark velvet. "If I have anything to say about it, one will most definitely not be enough."

Liquid tingles shot through her insides.

"I'll take care of it. Pick you up at six."

As Lacey saw it, her biggest problem was going to be how to face Clint after that bizarre phone conversation. Her face still flamed every time she thought about what she'd asked him. But what was a woman supposed to do? She'd been married to one man all her adult life. She'd never had to worry about modern dating problems before.

And Clint had laughed at her—and said he loved her.

He didn't mean it like that, you know he didn't.

Yes, she knew. But the echo of his words still had the power to stop her heart, to make her want things she had no business wanting.

One day at a time, Lacey girl, one day at a time.

Right. She wouldn't think about the future, only the now. And now, tonight, she and Clint would be together.

If he could quit laughing at her long enough.

If she didn't get cold feet and chicken out.

And what, she wondered, does one wear for an evening of farm chores, attack hens, and lovemaking?

TWELVE

At five-thirty Lacey was still wondering what to wear. She'd showered, washed, dried, and styled her hair, and had her makeup as perfect as she could get it. Ignoring the slight quaking in her stomach, she had painted her nails bright, sinful red. But what the devil should she wear? He'd liked the pink sundress, but he'd wanted her to go to the barn with him, and she hadn't been able to.

The only thing appropriate for the barn would be boots and jeans. Not exactly seductive. Unless . . . No, she couldn't. Could she? What would Clint think?

She imagined the look in his eyes when he saw what she was planning, and her knees turned to jelly.

Yes. To put a look like that in his eyes, she could do it. With trembling hands, she reached for the lingerie drawer.

She was barely dressed, just zipping her jeans, when she heard her parents come home. Damn. She'd hoped to be gone before they returned.

"Lacey, we're home. Are you here?"

Lacey opened her bedroom door. "I'm here, but I'm getting ready to leave," she called.

One more dab of Passion between her breasts, behind her ears, and she'd be ready.

"You say you're leaving?" her mother asked from the doorway.

"Yes." In the mirror, Lacey watched her mother's narrowed gaze follow the perfume bottle back to its spot on the dresser.

"Who with?"

Lacey clenched her jaws. Her mother hadn't asked the question, she'd demanded. *Demanded.*

"Who's the perfume for?"

Another demand.

"Lacey," her father called from the living room, "Clint's here."

She met her mother's gaze in the mirror. Pain? Pleading? Is that what she saw in her mother's eyes? Lacey blinked, and the look was gone. She picked up her purse and headed for the living room, her mother right behind her.

Clint heard her coming and had a smile ready. One look at her tight face, at Mrs. H.'s forbidding scowl, and his smile died.

"So where are you two going?"

Clint frowned. Damned if that didn't sound like a demand rather than a polite question. Before he could think of what to say, Lacey spoke.

"We're going out, Mama. Good night."

"Good night?" Mrs. H. cried. "Good night? What's that supposed to mean? When are you coming home?"

Lacey squeezed her eyes shut. "Mama, I'm a grown woman. I'll be home when I get home. Don't wait up."

"Lacey, honey, I just . . ."

"Your mother just doesn't want to see you make any more mistakes, sugarpie," Mr. H. said.

Clint had kept quiet as long as he could. He didn't particularly care for being considered a mistake. In fact, it really ticked him off. "What's going on here? Is there a problem I should know about?"

Lacey walked past him to the door. "Let's go, Clint."

"Problem!" her mother shrieked. "You know what the

problem is. You know what she's done to her life. What I don't understand is why you want anything to do with her. You heard what Charles said."

A sick feeling rolled through Clint's stomach. Behind him, Lacey made a strangled sound.

He looked from one parent to the other, his fists clenched. "I don't believe the two of you. Yeah, I heard what Charles said. And I'm ashamed to say I believed him, for a while. His story hit a little too close to home for comfort."

He looked over his shoulder at Lacey. Her face was too pale. "I got things a little mixed up in my mind," he said. "I started remembering things I shouldn't have, and I took it out on Lacey when she came home. As an excuse, it's not much."

He looked back to her parents. "But at least I know why I was fool enough to believe Charles. I can't for the life of me understand why her own parents would take his word as gospel and not listen to their own daughter."

"Listen to her?" Mrs. H. cried. "Listen to her call her own husband a liar?"

"He's her *ex*-husband, Mrs. H., and hell, yes, he's a liar. You know Lacey better than anyone in the world. How can you think she'd do the things he accused her of? Why would you even listen to him?"

"Forget it, Clint," Lacey said. "Their minds are made up. Don't confuse them with the truth. Let's get out of here." She pushed the screen door open and left.

"She's still our daughter," Mr. H. told him, "no matter how old she gets. You'll bring her home at a decent hour, won't you?"

"Frankly, Mr. H., with the atmosphere in this house, I can't imagine why she'd want to come home at all."

With that, Clint followed Lacey out the door. She stood beside the pickup, arms wrapped around her stomach, eyes downcast. "If you want to forget about tonight, I'll understand," she said.

"You might, but I won't." He tried to keep the anger

out of his voice. "You going to let them cheat us out of something we've both wanted for weeks?"

When she raised her head and looked at him, his throat ached. Her eyes were dull gray, glazed with pain. He willed her silently to see inside him, to know how much he wanted her. He wanted to take her in his arms right there in front of her parents. He wanted to make her pain go away.

Then slowly her eyes lightened. "They would be cheating us, wouldn't they?" Her lips curved. "I won't let them, if you won't."

His heart raced. "Not on your life, Ruffles." He ran a knuckle across her silky cheek. "Let's get out of here."

He opened the door for her and gave her a hand up into the pickup. He went around and crawled in behind the steering wheel, then reached out and grasped her hand. She hung on tight.

He smiled and backed out of the driveway. "What do you want to bet that I can think of something to take your mind off your troubles?"

She squeezed his fingers. Sadness laced the smile she gave him. "I wish you would."

They were quiet as he drove out of town. He didn't want to stop at the convenience store at Jacktown—the convenience store that *was* Jacktown—and buy biscuits and fried chicken for their dinner. If he stopped, he'd have to let go of her hand.

But he did stop. Before he turned loose of her, though, he brought her hand to his lips and kissed her knuckles. Her eyes flared.

"It worked," she whispered.

"What worked?" He kissed the inside of her wrist, his eyes never leaving hers.

"You took my mind off . . ."

His lips stole the rest of her words. "Good," he said against her mouth. "Hold that thought."

It took him less than three minutes to buy their supper and get back onto the highway toward the farm. For the rest of the ride, he watched her fidget with the strap of her purse and prayed she hadn't changed her mind.

At the farm, he ushered her inside the house and dropped the bag of chicken on the kitchen cabinet. He took her purse from her grasp and set it beside the chicken.

Then he took her in his arms and sighed. "I'm a selfish, jealous bastard."

"How so?" she asked against his neck.

He tipped her head until he could see her eyes. "Because I don't want you to think about Charles or your parents or anything else. I only want you to think about me. Even if it's just for tonight, I want to be the only one in your mind."

She reached her arms around his neck and said, "Then kiss me."

Sweet relief rushed through him. He brushed his lips against hers once, twice. She opened, he delved.

Lacey whimpered and clung to him, feeling the familiar heat of arousal burning inside her. He tasted dark, exciting. He smelled of spicy aftershave and clean, fresh air. Hungrily, she met his needs and claimed her own, pressing herself against him, feeling the hardness rise below his belt against her stomach.

Another whimper. Hers.

A low groan. His.

She tangled her fingers in his thick hair and felt him shiver. *Power.* She had the power to make this strong man shiver. This time the groan was hers. And the shiver.

He tore his lips from hers and spread kisses across her face. She gasped for breath.

"I want you," he said harshly against her ear.

She shivered again.

"I've wanted you since the night you came home." He burned a trail of kisses along her jaw. "You stood there in the tub, all gleaming and . . . wet. Your skin was so wet." His lips traced the length of her neck. "I want to make you that wet here," he whispered, his hand sliding around her hip and cupping her between her legs.

She cried out at his touch, his words. "I think . . . you just did." She pushed against his hand.

His hand pushed back. "Here? Inside?"

"Yes. Yes."

"Oh, God." He ran his hand up her fly and reached for the button. "I want to feel it. I want to touch your wetness, taste it."

Her knees buckled.

Clint swept her up in his arms and started for the guest bedroom, knowing his control was almost gone. She got to him faster than lightning. No one had ever made him lose his mind this way. The fire in her eyes scorched him. His breath rasped, his hands shook.

He laid her on the bed and followed her down, reaching for the buttons on her blouse as she undid his shirt. Her fingers burned his skin, took his breath, slowed him down. When he flipped her blouse open, he froze. "Oh, God, and it's not even my birthday."

Lacey saw the look in his eyes and smiled. She'd been right. That look was worth any amount of uncertainty she'd suffered. It filled her with elation, with power.

Her breasts, spilling from the top of the half-cup, black lace bra, swelled under the heat of his gaze.

Then he touched her, and her nipple peaked. His head lowered. She arched her back. "Yes," she whispered. "Please."

With a low growl, Clint flicked his tongue across the beaded point. She gasped. He kissed. She writhed. He suckled. She cried out.

She tasted like honey and felt like silk. He couldn't get enough of her. How was he going to get the rest of her clothes off without taking his mouth away?

After lavishing his attention on both breasts, he rose to his knees. With his gaze locked on hers, he tugged off her boots and socks, then his, then reached for her zipper.

Her eyes flamed.

He unzipped her jeans and tugged them down, then nearly collapsed when he saw the black lace triangle that matched her bra. He buried his face against the scratchy lace and inhaled. Lord help him, she'd put perfume beneath the lace. Something sweet and seductive that went straight to his head. And lower.

He kissed his way up her belly, her chest—*more perfume*—her neck, until he found her lips for a hungry, desperate kiss.

Lacey clung to him, thinking, *Yes, yes, this is right. This is how it's supposed to be.* She tugged his shirttail free and slid her eager palms up his broad back, following the curves and contours of hard muscles, her heart pounding more rapidly by the second. Sweat dampened his smooth skin; beads of it popped out at the base of his spine.

It wasn't enough. Not enough skin. She had to have more. Her lips still feasting on his, she tugged his shirt down his arms and tossed it aside.

Yes! Oh, his chest, his chest was beautiful to her fingers, sleek and firm and covered with whorls of crisp, tingly hair. His nipples felt as hard as her own. She flicked them with her nails.

Clint gasped and pulled his lips away. She wanted to protest, but couldn't. As he rose over her, she trailed her hands down his chest to the waistband of his jeans. He sucked in a sharp breath. With her fingernails, she traced the skin just above the denim, from his navel to his spine and back. Her gaze ate up his heaving chest, feasted on it, devoured it, then rose to meet his eyes.

They were hot. How could blue be so fiery?

With two fingers, he dipped into his front pocket and pulled out . . . a red foil pouch.

Lacey felt a flush rise from her breasts to her scalp. When he tucked the pouch into the palm of her hand, her face grew even hotter.

Then, with tortuous, teasing slowness, his knees still straddling her hips, he unsnapped his jeans. The tiny metallic *snick* echoed in her fevered brain and drew her gaze like steel filings to a magnet.

She gasped. The strained zipper looked ready to burst. Her lips felt parched. She licked them.

Clint made a harsh sound in his throat, then moved to stand beside the bed. When he shrugged off his jeans and white cotton briefs, she stared in awe. "You're beautiful."

His belly undulated, his body jerked. He crawled onto the bed and lay next to her, pulling her flush against his side. "Touch me. Please."

His tortured whisper twisted inside her belly. She rose on one elbow beside him, the foil packet pressing into her palm. She placed her other trembling hand in the middle of his tanned chest. The firm muscle quivered beneath her touch. She slid her hand downward.

Just below his waist, she stopped, and so did his tan. But even the paler skin of his hips was darker than her hand.

Clint tried not to squeeze her waist too hard. He tried not to beg. But if she didn't touch him soon, really touch him, he'd die.

Her heated gaze caressed him like a feather touch. It wasn't enough. He wanted those graceful, red-tipped fingers, that small, soft palm. "Touch me," he breathed.

But still she teased him, trailing her hand down one thigh, up the other, touching him everywhere but where he craved it, needed it. With the tips of her fingernails, she drove him crazy, raking the hair between his legs.

Closer. Her fingers trailed closer. He held his breath.

And then she touched him, and he jerked.

First a nail, sliding along him from tip to base. He shuddered with need.

Then one small finger. He was going to beg. Any second.

When she wrapped her hand around him, he groaned. His eyes slid shut, his hips rose. "Ah, Lacey."

She clasped him, gripped him, thrilled him. And nearly sent him over the edge.

"No more," he gasped.

Frantic to bury himself inside her, to feel himself totally surrounded, sliding into her, claiming her, making her his, he rolled her onto her back and nearly ripped her bra off before he found the clasp and freed it.

He touched her hungrily, everywhere, breathing in the sweet fragrance of her heated skin, tasting her flesh. The lace between her legs was no barrier at all. He merely nudged it aside and continued his touching, feeling, tasting, fulfilling his earlier wish.

Her thighs clenched, her belly rippled. The wanting, pleading sounds coming from her throat made him tighter, harder. So hard he ached.

He slid up her body and claimed her mouth again, dying a little when her arms and legs wrapped around him, cradling him in her warmth, her passion.

The condom. Lord, he had to remember the condom. Before it was too late. He rose to his knees, her thighs draped across his, and reached for the packet in her hand.

He had to wait, give himself a minute to calm a little, or he'd lose it. He let his eyes drink in her flesh. Her thighs were silky and pale against his. She lay there, open for him, reaching for him, her eyes a torment of need. The most vulnerable position a woman could ever be in. And it was for him.

Humbled, proud, he tore the packet open and handed the condom to her. "You do it," he whispered, his voice a mere breath.

Her eyes widened, startled. He wanted to follow her blush from the tips of her breasts upward with his lips. He didn't dare.

"I . . . I don't know how," she answered, her voice shaking.

Clint felt a melting in his heart. God, when was the last time a woman had said that to him—about anything! She didn't know *how?*

For a fleeting instant, female faces flashed through his mind. Pretty faces, some even beautiful. The faces of women he'd known intimately in recent years. Some younger than Lacey, some older. Not one of them had not known exactly what to do with a condom. Hell, most of them, even the nice, respectable ones, carried a supply in their purses.

One by one, those other faces disappeared, faster than they'd come. He knew in his gut he would never even want another woman from this moment on.

If he had ever had any lingering doubts about Lacey, about lovers she might or might not have had, they vanished, burned to cinders by her innocent admission, along with any question about exactly how he felt about her.

He'd been laughing when he told her over the phone earlier, but he wasn't laughing now. He'd meant it then. Now he meant it even more. He was deeply, desperately, irrevocably in love with Lacey Hamilton.

He took her hand in his and said, "Let me show you."

Her fingers trembled beneath his as he guided her through the process. When they finished, she touched him again, and the waiting was over.

He covered her with his body and sank into her, hard male flesh into feminine softness. Man to woman. Lover to lover.

He tried to go slow, make it last, but the moist heat of her flesh surrounding his, the movement of her hips beneath him, started a rhythm, ancient and primal, that took control of his body, his mind, his soul.

He soared, and she soared with him, through fire and darkness, through desperate passion, through the entwining of their spirits into the bursting lights and freedom of fulfillment. Their joint, breathless cries sang out together.

An eternity passed before Clint could open his eyes and roll to his side, taking Lacey with him. He was too stunned to do anything but gasp for breath and murmur her name. Nothing like Lacey had ever happened to him before.

He tilted her chin up, but her eyes were closed. "Lacey?"

Her lashes fluttered once, twice, then her lids raised, slowly, heavily.

His heart, which had yet to slow, galloped out of control again at what he saw in those soft gray depths. He saw in her eyes the same emotion that burned in his heart.

"You were right," she whispered.

His lips grazed hers. "About what?"

She closed her eyes and sighed, a deep, satisfied sigh that made his chest swell. "The earth did move."

Lacey woke to the dying rays of the sun streaking red through the crack between the drapes and the wall. She was alone. In the guest room at Clint's parents' house. For a moment, she panicked. Where was Clint?

From outside came frantic, irate cackling, followed by a low curse. The attack hens. Clint was doing the chores. She relaxed and smiled.

She really should be helping him. That's why she'd worn the boots and jeans. The boots and jeans that were now scattered somewhere on the floor.

With a soft moan, she stretched, relishing every delicious ache in her muscles. The sheets, the pillow, smelled of him. She closed her eyes and breathed in his scent.

She couldn't believe she'd fallen asleep, that she hadn't awakened when he'd left her side, when he'd tucked her beneath the covers. He was the most thoughtful man, taking care of her that way.

She should be just as thoughtful, and go help him with the chores. She kicked the covers aside and swung her legs off the bed. With a shriek, she jerked her feet back off the floor. Something crinkly had shifted beneath her toes!

Cautiously, blinking the sleep from her eyes, Lacey peered over the edge of the bed. Her eyes widened. Good gracious!

First she blushed. Then laughter started in her belly. Embarrassed laughter, delighted laughter. Hysterical laughter. It worked its way loose until it filled the room and made her sides ache.

What was it she had asked him? *Is one of those things going to be enough?*

How many were there? One, two, three, four . . . twelve! There on the floor beside the bed were twelve— *a full dozen!*—red foil packets, teasing her, taunting her, waiting to be opened and used.

"I told you one wouldn't be enough."

Startled by the sound of Clint's voice from the doorway, Lacey let out a squeak. "B-but a *dozen?*" she managed between gusts of laughter.

She pushed her hair back from her face and looked at him, still laughing too hard to think about being embarrassed.

But Clint wasn't laughing. Wasn't even smiling. At the look of intensity in his eyes, her own laughter died.

He leaned against the door frame and tugged off his boots and socks, his gaze never leaving hers. The heat from it licked at her belly. As he crossed the room to stand before her, he jerked off his shirt. Not an angry jerk. No, his eyes told her that. An impatient jerk.

Her heart thundered in a dozen places.

A dozen places, a dozen packets.

The thought made her skin tingle, her lips curve upward. He stood before her, nostrils flaring like some beast sniffing the wind for a mate. As far as Lacey was concerned, Clint had just found his. She reached for the snap of his jeans. "If you plan to use them all tonight, we'd better get started."

Then Clint burst out laughing. He dropped to his knees in front of her, between her own knees, and buried his face against her breasts. Then he said those words again. "God, Lacey, I love you."

But as before, he was laughing.

He cupped her face in both hands. When his mouth took hers, she forgot. Forgot he didn't really mean the words. Forgot there was a world outside his arms. Forgot everything. Except the sound of the metal teeth of a zipper slowly releasing their grip on each other. The sound of another foil packet being ripped open.

His hands left her for a moment, then settled on her waist. "Come here," he said with a growl.

He pulled her off the bed until she straddled his hips where he knelt on the floor. Then with a slowness that was agonizing, he filled her.

Clint groaned and buried himself inside her. "I may never get enough of you."

He'd told himself while he'd been outside that his mind had played tricks on him. What he'd thought he'd felt earlier in her arms, the sheer intensity of emotions and physical satisfaction, could not have been so shattering.

He'd been wrong.

THIRTEEN

When Lacey woke the next morning, alone in her own bed, the first emotion that swelled in her chest was sheer, unadulterated terror. She was in love with Clint Sutherland.

If she had been paying closer attention to her own mind and heart instead of denying her feelings, she would have known it sooner. And she would never have gone with him last night.

But Lord help her, last night had been the most . . . she didn't know what word to use. Incredible didn't come close. Overwhelming was more like it.

She'd had no idea a man and woman could generate such intense emotions, such heat within each other, and not go up in flames.

With her face buried in her pillow, she swore. She didn't want to be in love. She'd only been fooling herself when she thought she could take things with Clint one day at a time. Now, heaven help her, she had visions of rocking babies in Grandmother Sutherland's cherrywood rocker.

A deep ache settled in her gut. What was she going to do? If she continued seeing him, she knew her feelings would only grow. But would not seeing him make them disappear?

Not likely. She was in too deep.

When she thought of how much of herself she had revealed to him last night, how much she had given, taken, shared, she wanted to cry. Clint was a perceptive man, but even an imbecile could have seen her heart in her eyes.

So maybe she wouldn't have to worry about what to do. Maybe, if he realized how she felt, he would break it off between them. Maybe he'd run as far and fast from her as he could. After all, a man who laughs hysterically when he says "I love you" does *not* want to be taken seriously.

When she crawled out of bed, her muscles protested. What last night had been a delicious reminder of glorious lovemaking, now only hurt. She'd been a fool. She had no business falling in love with Clint or any other man. She had a life to get back on track.

And before another day went by, she intended to somehow make peace with her parents. More specifically, her mother. Dad would go along with whatever Mama suggested. But Mama wasn't going to be easy.

After a shower, Lacey walked through the house and discovered she was the only one around. Her parents had gone out somewhere. She poured herself a cup of coffee and a bowl of Cheerios, then sat at the table to read the latest edition of the *Deep Fork Weekly*.

A small headline near the bottom of the front page caught her eye: WILL DEEP FORK'S MAYOR RUN?

With every word of the short column, Lacey's blood turned a little colder. Clint was being urged to run for the State House of Representatives. Judging from the quotes in the article, he was seriously considering it, and was likely to win if he ran.

Lacey dropped her spoon into the cereal. Milk and Cheerios splattered the table. He couldn't! Lord, why had she ignored the teasing comments she'd heard at the café?

She never, *never* would have allowed herself to fall for him had she known what he was planning.

Not Clint. Please, not Clint.

He *couldn't* run for representative. How could this be happening? Sure, others had commented, but Clint had laughed off suggestions that he might run. Why hadn't he told her, damn him?

He couldn't spend every day at the state capital, in the same building with Charles Johnston, hearing Charles's lies. Lord, if Charles found out Clint was seeing her . . . The damage to Clint's reputation would be total. Charles would stop at nothing to discredit her, and anyone associated with her.

She let out her breath and stared at the steam rising from her coffee.

Well. That was it, then. If she had had doubts earlier about her relationship with Clint, she didn't have any now. There could be no relationship with Clint. Not for her. Not now, not ever. Not if he ran for representative.

The newspaper crumpled in her fist. She closed her eyes against the pain in her chest. By the time her parents came in a half hour later carrying bags of groceries, Lacey hadn't moved.

"You're finally up," her mother said. "Help me put these groceries away, then I want to talk to you."

Lacey didn't have the strength to argue. With stiff, jerky movements, she rose to comply. When the groceries were put up and the paper bags folded and stored in the pantry, Lacey dumped her cereal down the garbage disposal and wiped the table off.

"Sit down, honey," Irma said. "I want to talk to you."

Whatever it was, Lacey knew she didn't want to hear it. But numbness was settling in, and her mind was going blank. Wonderfully blank. Walking out of the room would take too much effort just now, and might jar her brain into functioning again. Mustn't have that. Didn't want to think, didn't want to feel.

She sat across from Irma. She would hear what her

mother had to say, then maybe she'd go for a walk. The woods at the end of the street would be nice this time of year, filled with new growth, nesting birds, and bunnies. A pleasant diversion.

"Honey," Irma said. She placed a work-worn hand on Lacey's.

Lacey flinched. It was the first time her mother had touched her since the half-hearted hug they'd shared Easter Sunday. The touch was both familiar and alien. But the familiarity was from long ago. The only one to touch her in recent months, the only human touch she'd received, was from Clint.

And oh, what Clint's touching had done. He'd touched her body, her heart, even her soul, in a way no man had ever done.

Don't think about Clint.

Right. She wouldn't think about him. She raised her gaze to her mother's face. "What did you want to talk about, Mama?"

Irma took a deep breath. "About you and Clint."

"No." Lacey swallowed and pulled her hand free. "I don't want to talk about Clint."

"Lacey, honey, I know you're . . . attracted to him. And I imagine, judging by how close to sunup you came home this morning, that it's already too late for me to tell you not to get involved with him. You're having an affair, aren't you."

Lacey stiffened. That last had not been a question, but a bald statement.

"I know you're a little lost right now," Irma continued before Lacey could respond. "You're trying to find your way into a new life, because you've decided you didn't like the old one. But, Lacey, getting involved with another man is not the answer."

Lacey gave a wry chuckle. "I suppose you're going to tell me what the answer is? The secret to a happy life."

"I can tell you what it isn't. It isn't running blindly

from one man to the next. I don't want to see you get hurt, honey.''

"Ha! That's a laugh. The only one hurting me around here is you, Mama.''

Irma blinked rapidly. "I don't mean to, honey, but I can't stand by and watch you ruin your life. Have you even *tried* to talk to Charles these past months? You belong with him, you know. With Charles, not Clint.''

Lacey felt the fury come, and she relished it. It surged in her blood and warmed the icy places in her heart. "I will not sit here and listen to you tell me anything about Charles Johnston. The man is a vicious liar, and that's the *nicest* thing I can say about him.''

"You have no right—''

"I have every right, Mama.'' Lacey clenched her fists on the table top. "You're the one who has no right. You can't run my life, can't tell me who I should see, who I shouldn't. And you can't keep telling me I belong with *that man.*''

Her mother's jaw firmed. "As long as you're my daughter, as long as you live under this roof, I do have the right. I'm going to call Charles on the phone, and you're going to talk with him and try to straighten out your problems.''

Lacey was stunned beyond belief. "The hell you are!''

"How dare you use such language to me, young lady!''

"My language? *My* language? The words that just came out of your mouth are ten times more foul than any curse I could come up with. You really, sincerely believe—''

"I really, sincerely believe that as long as you're my daughter, as long as you live in this house, you have to at least listen to what I say.''

Lacey felt as though a huge vice were clamping down on her chest. She couldn't stand it any more, the hurtful, persistent betrayal, the accusations.

Then tell her the truth. Tell her the real reason for your divorce.

But she couldn't. The words wouldn't come. And as

loyal as her mother was being to the Charles she thought she knew, Irma wasn't likely to believe the truth.

No. Lacey should *not* have to defend herself, dammit! Her resolve hardened. "I can't do anything about being your daughter," she said, "but I can damn sure do something about living in this house." Lacey shoved back her chair and stood up.

"What do you mean?"

"I mean I can't—*won't*—put myself through this any more. I should have known better than to come here. But then, how could I?" she added with a sharp laugh. "How could I have known my own mother would think I'm some kind of misguided tramp?"

Irma's face turned red. "Well, who else would leave a kind, loving husband—an important state senator—for another man?"

Lacey leaned over the table, her fists clenched. "For the last time, Mama—I did *not* leave Charles for another man!"

"Then you tell me, missy, just where you were for six months, if not with the man you'd been seeing?"

"I wasn't seeing any man!"

"Then who were you spending your weekends with right before you left town?"

Lacey reared back, confused, both by the words, and by the surprised, guilty blush on her mother's cheeks. Lacey's stomach rolled with suspicion. "What," she managed between clenched teeth, "are you talking about?"

Her mother let out a heavy sigh. With her hands over her face, she said, "I wasn't supposed to say anything. I promised Charles I wouldn't."

The suspicion in Lacey's stomach turned to dread. "I think you'd better tell me what the devil you're talking about."

Irma lowered her hands. "Yes. I guess it's time. Maybe then you'll finally realize how I know Charles wasn't lying the day he came out here. You might want to sit down."

Yes, Lacey agreed. She suddenly felt an overwhelming

need to sit down, if for no other reason than to keep from running out. Out of the house, out of town. Out of the whole damn state of Oklahoma. Whatever her mother was about to tell her, Lacey knew with sickening certainty that she didn't want to hear it.

She sat down.

"He called here, Lacey," Irma said, a look of . . . was that pity in her eyes? "Charles called three times during the month before you wrote and said the two of you were divorcing."

Irma sat back in her chair, brows raised as if waiting for a response.

Lacey shrugged. It wasn't unusual for Charles to call her parents. "So?"

Irma shook her head. "You're going to make me say it, aren't you?"

Lacey ground her teeth in frustration. "I still don't know what your talking about."

"Honey." Irma rested her hand on Lacey's. "He called here looking for you after you told him you were spending the weekend with us."

"What do you mean?" Lacey pulled her hand free. "I never told him—"

"Three weekends in a row. And of course, you were never here."

"Of course I wasn't here. I was at home." A sudden feeling of horror engulfed her. "You mean he thought I was—no, he *said* I was supposed to be staying with you?"

Irma nodded. Creases of worry lined her brow.

Lacey shook her head in wonder, a dreamlike feeling of unreality settling over her. Charles was even more devious that she had imagined. What reason could he possibly have had for going to all that trouble? "I don't understand."

"What's to understand?" Irma asked quietly. "You lied to him about where you were spending the weekends, and he found out."

Reality returned in a rush, and with it, rage. Lacey

welcomed it. She slammed a fist against the table. "I didn't lie to him, dammit. I didn't go anywhere! I was right in my own home, and he knew it."

Irma reared back with a gasp. "I can't believe you're denying this! You're caught, Lacey June. Why don't you just admit it?"

Eyes wide, clammy sweat forming across her skin, Lacey rose slowly from her chair and glared at her mother, her whole body trembling with rage. "That is absolutely the last time you will *ever* call me a liar, Mama. If you choose to believe the word of that bastard without asking my side of things, that's your problem. Had you bothered to call the house any of those weekends, you'd have known Charles was lying, because I probably would have answered the damn phone myself."

Not wanting for a response, Lacey headed for her room.

"Where are you going?" her mother cried.

Lacey didn't answer. When she got to her room, she yanked her empty suitcase from beneath the bed and started filling it. She tossed wads of underwear and handfuls of cosmetics in haphazardly, then started jerking clothes from the closet.

"You're not leaving!" her mother cried. "Lacey, we can talk about it."

"Talk about what?" she asked, her voice as cold as the blood in her veins. "Talk about how you believe everything Charles told you? About what a bad girl I've been? About what I should do to straighten myself out? No thank you, Mama."

When the suitcase was full, Lacey slapped it shut and fastened the latch, then grabbed her purse and car keys and brushed past her mother.

"Where are you going?"

Was that a quiver of emotion in her mother's voice? No, surely it was only Lacey's imagination. "None of your business," she said firmly.

"Lacey, honey—"

"I'm going to go find the nearest man to run off with, Mama, is that what you want to hear?"

"I don't believe you."

"Why not? You think I've done it before."

Lacey slammed out the front door and headed for the curb, where her father had parked her car so he could have the double garage to himself. With a sudden lump in her throat, she threw her suitcase into the back seat.

Irma had stayed at the front door. Now she called back into the house, "Neal, Neal! Come quick. Lacey's leaving!"

Isn't that what you wanted, Mama?

Lacey jammed the key into the ignition and cranked the old Datsun to life. A cloud of exhaust billowed behind her as she tore away from the curb and down the street. At Main, she turned left, not having any idea where she was headed. It didn't matter. Just as long as she got away.

She gripped the steering wheel until her knuckles turned white, trying to keep her violent shaking under control.

She was passing Sutherland's Feed and Seed, her eyes grimly refusing to look at anything but the highway before her, when a horn honked. Out of reflex, she looked over. Her heart squeezed. It was Clint.

He stepped out of his pickup with a big smile and a wave.

Tears stung her eyes. She tried to smile back, so he wouldn't know anything was wrong. Heaven forbid he should come after her. She wouldn't be able to deal with that at all. She managed a tight little wave.

His smile faded, his brow furrowed.

Lacey jerked her gaze back to the road and drove on. He didn't need her in his life, and she refused to need him.

At the edge of town, she hit the gas. The poor little Datsun whined and chugged down the highway.

Clint watched Lacey drive out of town, wondering where she was going, puzzled by the expression he'd seen on her face. He'd expected a smile. Needed it. The one he got was half-hearted, at best.

Then he grinned crookedly. After last night, he couldn't blame her for feeling a little shy. His heart raced just remembering how perfect their joining had been each and every time they'd made love.

He slammed the door of the pickup and headed for the storeroom, shaking his head, biting back a grin. They'd put a serious dent in his supply of red foil packets.

At the thought, heat knifed straight to his loins.

He couldn't wait to see her again, touch her, hold her, kiss her. As soon as he cleaned up after work, he'd go straight to the café. He couldn't hold her or touch her or kiss her there, but, he thought with another grin, he could at least watch her walk in those skin-tight denims.

Must be love, he thought, surprised at the calm acceptance he felt. He hadn't realized and would never have admitted he was ready to fall in love again. But with Lacey, being ready had nothing to do with it. He didn't have a choice. It had already happened. Weeks ago.

And what was he planning to do about it?

Whatever it took, he decided. Whatever it took to keep her beside him, to see her rock a child—his child—in his grandmother's chair, to watch her hair turn from gold to silver over the years. He wanted it all.

And he'd read those same wants in her eyes last night. She was his. He knew it—she knew it.

He couldn't wait to see her again.

Lacey made it three whole miles from town before her blurred vision forced her to pull off the road. She didn't want to leave this way. She *liked* living in Deep Fork. She had friends there, roots.

Her heart was there.

Her nose stung while her chin and lower lip quivered uncontrollably.

Damn, she didn't want to cry! But the tears didn't care because they came anyway. She forced them back to an occasional trickle, knowing she had to decide, here and now, exactly what to do.

She didn't want to leave, but she couldn't live in the same house with her mother another hour, couldn't take another one of those condemning looks. Neither could she bring herself to tell what really happened between her and Charles. Dammit, she shouldn't have to! Her parents should have believed in her!

Then there was Clint to consider. Loving him only complicated everything. Why hadn't she paid more attention to local gossip? Why had she let herself fall in love with a man with his eye on a legislative seat? A man whose life was about to take a dramatic turn? A man who didn't need her, who said he loved her, but laughed while saying it? A man who could set her on fire with just a look. . . .

That was a large part of her urge to flee, she admitted. Around Clint, she lost control of her body, her very thoughts, at a time in her life when she wanted desperately to re-establish the control she had relinquished to Charles years ago.

So there she sat, on the side of State Highway 177, knowing she should keep heading south toward the interstate, with her heart crying to turn around.

And if she hit the interstate, then what? She had barely enough money to last a week, with nowhere to go. In Deep Fork, at least she had a job. It wasn't much, and it might be temporary, but it was a job.

Maggie and Mort would be hurt and disappointed at her leaving this way, with no word, no notice.

She pictured the old café with its worn linoleum floor, grease stained ceiling and rattling air conditioner and smiled sadly. She would miss it.

Then she frowned. Something about the café, something she should remember tickled her mind and made her pulse race. But what?

She tried to shake off the feeling, but it persisted. Something she'd heard? Something Maggie had said, something to do with the cash register.

Suddenly it hit her, and she shivered in the hot car.

The garage apartment behind the café. Maggie had offered her the use of it. The key was under the cash tray in the register.

Could she do it? Could she live in that apartment, work in the café, knowing how often she would see Clint and her parents if she stayed in town?

At least in Deep Fork she had Maggie. If she left, she'd have no one, nothing. But if she left, she wouldn't have to worry about seeing Clint, wanting him, staying away from him.

Coward!

In the end, the lure of seeing Clint, if only by serving him dinner at the café, was stronger than her urge to run. Somehow her mind must have already made the decision, for when she wiped her eyes dry, she was headed north on the highway, back to Deep Fork, and the ancient Datsun was humming along smoothly at sixty miles an hour.

At the edge of town, where the Deep Fork Wildcats' paw prints started their march past the feed store toward the high school, she slowed to the required thirty-five and breathed a sigh of relief. Clint wasn't outside any longer.

She pulled her car up behind the café and went in through the kitchen. Mort looked up from the grill in surprise. "Early, aren't you?"

"Just passing through," she told him.

In the dining room, she waited while Maggie said goodbye to the only customer, then made her way to the cash register.

"Hiya," Maggie said. "What are you doing here this time of day?"

Lacey opened the register, lifted the cash tray, and pulled out the keys Maggie had told her about. She dangled them from her finger. "Is one for the garage?"

Maggie frowned. "Yes. The big one. What's happened?"

"You didn't see me take these. You don't have any idea where I am. Right?"

With a hesitant nod, Maggie agreed. "You wanna talk about it?"

A lump formed in Lacey's throat. "Not . . . not yet. Thanks, Magoo," she said with a wave of the keys. "You don't know how much this means to me."

Maggie gave her a hug. "Anytime, you know that. Just take it easy, huh? And if you need anything, holler. I'm always here for you."

"I know." Lacey felt her chin start to quiver. She gave a sniff, then said, "See you at four."

She dashed through the kitchen and waved a quick good-bye to Mort. Before checking out her new home, she put her car in the garage, grabbed her suitcase, and made sure the big barn-type doors were securely locked. She didn't want her car visible. The longer she could keep her whereabouts a secret from her parents and Clint, the better.

Suitcase in hand, she studied the rickety stairs leading to the apartment. A zillion splinters made the banister resemble some misshapen porcupine. The second step from the bottom looked rotten. The third step from the top sported a rusty nail, sharp end sticking out at least two inches. She would need a hammer.

Taking a deep breath and a deathlike grip on her suitcase, Lacey started up, one cautious step at a time. She skipped the stair that looked rotten, kept her free hand away from the wicked-looking banister, and sidestepped the protruding nail.

At the top of the stairs, she put the key into what passed for a lock, realizing with a wry grin that this would be the first apartment she'd ever had—the first time (with the exception of her six-month stint as a house-sitter for her cousin) that she had lived alone. She turned the key and pushed the door open. Her wry grin turned into a grimace.

What had Maggie said?

The apartment's certainly no decorator showplace . . .

Good ol' Maggie. Lacey never realized her best friend was such a master at understatement.

The once-white walls of the front room had yellowed with age. Before a draped window overlooking the alley sat a sagging divan covered—at least in most places—with worn, brown corduroy. An olive drab recliner sitting at right angles to the divan was the only "color" in the room, except for a red fringed lamp on the scarred end table.

No. Not a decorator showplace. More like a classic portrait in Early Tacky. Or maybe Depression Attic.

Depressing Attic.

Lacey set her suitcase on the beige and brown floral carpet. Gad. Beige and brown flowers?

The kitchen, bedroom, and bath were each *almost* large enough to accommodate one person. Lacey had a feeling that if she ate too many more of Mort's cheeseburgers, she just might get herself stuck in the rusty shower stall. She didn't have to worry about the bathtub, though—there wasn't one.

"Well, here I am," she told the apartment. "Home, sweet home."

At six-thirty, Clint stepped out his front door and walked with eager strides to the café. To Lacey. He tucked his fingertips into his front pockets and laughed at himself. He hadn't felt such a heady rush of anticipation, of eagerness at seeing a female, since his teens.

The bell over the café door jingled merrily, echoing his mood. Like a bee to clover, his gaze zeroed in on Lacey. She was setting a plate down in front of a stranger on the far side of the room. That was apparently her side tonight, so he took the empty booth beside the stranger and waited impatiently for her to notice him.

Would she blush? She'd blushed a time or two last night, he remembered with a grin.

He heard the typical clattering of dishes from the kitchen, then, what seemed like an eternity later, she came out. He took one look at her drawn face and tensed.

She looked up and saw him. He sent her a secret smile.

She didn't return it. Instead, the most unbelievable thing happened. She came to a jerking halt, and the blood drained from her face, leaving her pale as a ghost.

Something was wrong. Drastically, terribly wrong. Her face and his gut told him so.

"Hey, Clint!" Harvey Cornwallis from the drugstore slipped into Clint's booth.

Reluctantly, Clint tore his gaze from Lacey's white face. "Hey, Harvey, how's it going?"

Harvey launched into a monologue on all the things he'd like to see Clint accomplish if elected to the House. During the endless list of necessary bridge repairs, more jobs for the district, more state funding for education—all things Clint had been highly aware of for years, things he meant to aim for if elected—Lacey brought water and menus to the table. She nodded to Harvey, but never looked at Clint before speeding away. She didn't come back, either. Harriet came to take his and Harvey's orders.

Harvey rambled on, and Clint managed to give an occasional nod and grunt of agreement, all the while watching Lacey. His dinner, when Harriet brought it, tasted like cardboard. Lacey never came back to his side of the room.

What had happened, he wondered, to make her react like that to seeing him? A sharp sense of panic had him deserting Harvey in the middle of another of his long-winded monologues. Clint had to talk to Lacey. *Now*. If it meant cornering her in the kitchen, so be it.

But before he reached the kitchen door, Lacey came out. With a startled gasp, she turned back toward the kitchen.

"Lacey." Clint grabbed her arm and stopped her. "Look at me, dammit. What's wrong?"

But she wouldn't look at him. Her gaze darted wildly, as if seeking a quick escape.

"I can't talk now, Clint, I'm working."

"Just tell me what's wrong. What's happened?"

Her shoulders heaved. Then she finally looked at him— not eye to eye, but at least he could see her face. She flashed him what he assumed was supposed to be a smile. The brittle falseness of it sent dread and anger coursing through him.

"Nothing's happened," she claimed with forced brightness. "What could have happened?" She stepped out of his grasp. "I've got to get back to work."

Clint wanted to stop her. He wanted to drag her off somewhere private and demand she tell him what the hell was going on. But a quick glance told him he and Lacey were drawing way too much attention.

He let her go.

She turned back toward the kitchen.

"Lacey?" he called.

She stopped, but didn't face him.

"Whatever's wrong, I'm not letting it drop. We'll talk later. All right?"

After a pause, she nodded stiffly. "All right. Later."

When she disappeared through the swinging door, Clint had the sickening feeling she was also disappearing from his life.

What the hell had happened? Last night had been . . . perfect. He'd stake his life that she had thought so, too. Now this.

Clint's earlier sense of panic mushroomed. He found himself paying for his meal and escaping the café as quickly as possible, his mind scurrying for reasons for her actions. None came.

He couldn't leave things as they were. He had promised her they would talk, and talk they would. At ten o'clock he stood across the street and watched the last customer leave the café. On the chance that she might try to avoid him as she had earlier, Clint decided to wait in the shadows for Lacey to come out. When she crossed the street toward home, he would step out and demand an explanation.

Harriet turned the sign in the door to read "Closed." By ten-thirty, she was out the door and Mort's big form was locking it behind her. Where was Lacey?

Harriet walked around the corner to the side street and left in her car. The lights in the café went out. A moment later, Mort's old station wagon rumbled out of the back alley and rolled away up Main.

Where was Lacey? Had she gone out the back door, knowing he would be out front?

Clint sprinted across the street, around the corner to the alley behind the café. It was dark. The corner street light didn't reach there. Nothing moved. The alley was empty. Where the devil could she have gone? And *why*, dammit?

He walked all the way around the old garage with its upstairs apartment, feeling stupid. Lacey wouldn't hide in the damn alley, and no one in her right mind would get within twenty feet of the dilapidated garage. If it weren't for the brick buildings along Main, the thing would have blown down years ago in a stiff breeze.

Lacey must have gone out the back and around the block without his seeing her. Maybe he could still catch her. He dashed back to the corner, then across Main. But when he turned on his street, it was deserted. No lights shone at the Hamilton house.

What the hell kind of game was she playing? Anger warred with his confusion and pain. All three stayed with him through the night and the next day. He was determined to find out what was going on in that mind of hers.

By noon, his patience was gone. He left Jeff Bonner in charge of the store and stomped all the way up the hill and down the block to the house next door to his. Mr. and Mrs. H. were both out front working in the flower beds.

"Hello, Clint," Irma called.

Clint stuffed his hands in his front pockets and nodded. "Mrs. H." He nodded to her and Mr. H. "I've come to talk to Lacey. She inside?"

The look the two shared made Clint's nape prickle. "What is it?"

"She's not here," Mrs. H. said. She pushed herself up from the ground and faced him.

"Where'd she go? I really need to talk to her."

"We . . . don't know where she went. She just took off. She's left us, Clint. Packed her clothes into her car and left us."

Clint felt his heart lurch. "Why? What happened? When did she leave?"

Mr. H. came slowly to his feet and put his arm around his wife's shoulders. "Yesterday afternoon," he said.

"It was my fault," Mrs. H. said tearfully. "I was just trying to make her see how she was ruining her life . . ."

Clint squeezed his eyes shut for a moment, despair washing over him. "You argued about Charles, right?"

Mrs. H. nodded. "Now she's gone, and we don't know where. She was so upset, she may never come back. We may never see her again."

"Of course you'll see her again. Just walk over to the café. What can she do, throw you out?"

Mr. H. dropped his arm from his wife's shoulders and took a hesitant step forward. "What . . . the café? What do you mean? She's left town, Clint. Gone."

Clint frowned. "She was working at the café last night."

The two looked at each other, stunned. Clint shook his head. "You mean you thought she'd left town for good? What did she say? What . . . no, never mind. If you started in on her again about Charles, I'm surprised she *didn't* leave town."

"Clint! How can you say that?" Mrs. H. cried. Then she narrowed her eyes. "But then it's to your advantage for her to keep on with her wild ways, isn't it?"

Clint stiffened. He rammed his clenched fists into his pockets to keep from . . . from what? Hitting the woman? No, but a good, hard shake wouldn't hurt.

"Irma," Mr. H. cautioned.

"Is that what you think, Mrs. H? That I'm just the next man in line for Lacey?" Clint paused. The trembling rage in his gut threatened to overwhelm him. "God, no wonder she left home. You're fools, both of you, if you can't see through Johnston's lies.''

Clint whirled and stormed down the sidewalk, furious with Lacey's parents, hurting for her.

But that still didn't explain her actions last night. He couldn't help remembering the feel of her, the taste, the way she touched him and took his breath away. She couldn't have forgotten what they had shared.

So why had she looked at him last night as if he were the neighborhood axe murderer?

This time he wouldn't try to confront her in the café, wouldn't give her any warning that he was near. At ten o'clock that night, he peered through the window of the café and made certain she was inside. She was.

He stood across the street and waited. From there, he could see if she went out the front, and he had a plain view of the back door.

''You're not sneaking away from me this time, Ruffles.''

FOURTEEN

With a mixture of sadness and relief, Lacey stepped out into the back alley with Mort, then waved as he drove away. Clint hadn't come tonight. But wasn't that for the best? Looking at him, even just thinking of him, remembering the way it had been the night they'd made love . . . knowing it could never happen again, gave her such a hopeless feeling.

Tonight he hadn't come. She hadn't seen him, hadn't heard his voice or been in the same room with him. Still, she'd thought of him constantly. Every time the front door opened, she'd jumped, fearing—hoping?—it was him.

Fool. She didn't *want* to see him. He wanted to know what was wrong, what had happened.

How could she ever explain?

Careful to keep her hand off the splintery banister, she climbed the stairs beside the old garage to the apartment above. Her new home. Just the thought of spending another night, then another, in this dismal, lonely place put a lump in her throat.

Then she remembered why she was here rather than with her parents. While her mother's treatment of her hurt, even enraged Lacey, it also strengthened her determina-

188

tion. She pushed the key into the lock even a child could pick and pushed open the door.

Behind her came a creak of sound, a breath. Nerves on sudden alert, she whirled.

"I told you we were going to talk."

Lacey's heart slammed against her rib cage. Clint! He'd nearly scared the life out of her. "What are you doing here?" she demanded. Fear put a harshness in her voice. "How did you . . ." Bad question. It would sound like she'd been hiding from him.

Well, it's the truth.

"How did I find you?"

Heat stung Lacey's cheeks. "What do you want?" Another bad question.

He reached around her and pushed the door open. "For starters, an explanation."

Clint was so close, she could feel the heat from his body. Shaken, she stepped into the room and flipped on the light. It was a mistake. He followed her. She hugged her purse to her chest and took another step away.

He clasped her shoulder. "Lacey—"

She jerked from his touch and whirled to face him. "Why didn't you tell me you were running for state representative?"

"I didn't come here to talk about that," he said with a scowl. "I came to talk about you and me."

"I *am* talking about you and me."

He looked surprised, confused.

Realizing she must look like a frightened mouse, hugging her purse to her chest and cowering before him, Lacey tossed her purse onto the couch and straightened her shoulders. "Why didn't you tell me?"

"I honestly didn't think of it." He planted his hands on his hips. "I haven't made up my mind yet, anyway. Is this why you're acting like I've got the plague? Because I might run for the legislature?" He took a step closer to her.

Lacey stood her ground and looked him in the eye, her

heart thundering, breaking, her voice firm. "I won't have anything to do with a politician."

His eyes widened, then narrowed to dangerous slits. "That didn't stop you from crawling into bed with the mayor of this town, dammit."

Score one direct hit for his side. Lacey swallowed hard. "That's different. It's not the same as being a state representative."

"I'm trying to understand this. You mean city hall is okay, but the state capitol isn't?"

When put like that, Lacey admitted it sounded weak.

"This has something to do with Charles, doesn't it?" Clint demanded. He was getting angry. She could tell by the narrowed eyes, the flaring nostrils. She looked away, unable to meet his gaze. How could she tell him— She couldn't. She wouldn't know where to begin, what to say.

"I'm right, aren't I?" Clint asked coldly. "You don't want anything to do with a man who might end up being around your ex-husband." A muscle in his jaw flexed. "You think if I'm around him I'll start believing his lies again, is that it?"

"No!" she cried. "But he's bound to repeat them if he learns you have anything to do with me. It's . . . better if we just call it quits now, before we get in any deeper."

"You can do that?" he demanded. "You can just turn off your feelings?"

"Clint—"

"What if I don't run? What then?"

She shook her head. She didn't know what to tell him.

"Are you saying I have to choose between you and the legislature?"

"No! Clint, no. I'd never ask you to choose."

"That's good," he said. He walked forward until their bodies nearly touched. "Because I happen to think I can handle both."

"It doesn't matter," she told him. "We . . . we moved too fast. I'm not ready to get involved. I've got—"

"Not ready?" he cried. "If the other night wasn't involved, I don't know what the hell is."

"It shouldn't have happened!"

"But it did. Now you want to forget it?"

"That's right."

A dangerous glint came to his eyes. "Not on your life, Ruffles. Neither one of us will ever forget, and you know it."

Then he kissed her. Hard and deep, with his arms wrapping around her, pressing her to him.

Don't do this, she screamed silently. *Don't touch me, don't kiss me. Don't make me feel this way.*

She clung to him, knowing she was crazy. She had to break it off. Instead, she kissed him back. When she was breathless, aching with wanting him, he pulled away.

"Try to forget *that*, Ruffles. I dare you."

He left her there and slammed the door on his way out.

She stood for several moments staring at the door. She wished she knew what she was doing, what she was supposed to do. Wished she knew what had just happened. And how she was supposed to live her life without him.

Her eyes burned, but the tears wouldn't fall.

Try to forget . . .

She knew she wouldn't. She would never forget his touch, his kiss, the breathless way he made her feel. Not for the rest of her life.

During the next couple of weeks Lacey's prediction proved more than true. How could she forget her feelings for Clint when he wouldn't stay away from her? He showed up every night at the café for dinner, then sat around visiting with friends for at least another hour. Time and again she was forced to wait on him, serve his food, refill his tea. Hear his voice. See his smile.

After the first few times, she slowly learned to control her reaction to him. By the end of a week, she was almost able to look him in the eye. Almost. She was finally able to ask him for his order without her voice quivering, though. That progress, however small, was welcomed.

At least she could be grateful that her parents didn't come to the café while she was working. And she was grateful. She was also more than a little hurt. They had to know where she was, but they made no effort to contact her.

Lacey slogged through her days, worked evenings, and tossed and turned most of each night. Her dreams alternated between nightmares about arguing with her mother to dreams of Clint that left her hot and aching inside, wanting him. She couldn't decide which were worse, the dreams or the nightmares, but between them, she dreaded falling asleep.

Maggie and Mort both worried about her, she knew. They saw her pick at her meals, looked at the dark circles beneath her eyes, and clucked their tongues.

Lacey worked hard at avoiding their sharp gazes. But eventually, during shift change on a Thursday afternoon, Maggie cornered her at the ice bin. "It must be love," Maggie said.

Lacey gave a start and felt a blush sting her cheeks. "Love? Me? You've got to be kidding." She jammed the scoop into the crushed ice. "I don't have time to fall in love."

"Yeah, right. Problem is, love doesn't wait for a convenient time. It's got its own timetable, and mere humans that we are, we can't do a thing about it."

"I told you, I'm not in love." She dumped the scoopful of ice into a pitcher.

"Yeah, right. That's why you tighten up like a cinch every time a certain mayor walks through the door."

"Don't be ridiculous."

"Besides. What else other than love can make a person so miserable?" Maggie crossed her arms and blocked Lacey's escape route.

Lacey scooped more ice into the pitcher. Her shoulders sagged. "I can't argue with that. Love stinks."

Maggie gave a hearty laugh. "I was right! You're in love with Clint, aren't you?"

"It doesn't matter." The pitcher was full. Lacey dropped the scoop back into the ice bin. "I'll just have to get over it."

Maggie smirked. "Yeah, right."

"Leave it alone, Maggie, please."

"You're obviously pushing him away. I think you're making a mistake."

"How can you say that? You don't know what's going on."

"I know what I hear, I know what I see with my own eyes. The man is crazy about you."

"So maybe I'm not crazy about him."

"Who are you trying to kid? I'm your best friend, and I love you. But, Lacey, you never used to lie to yourself this way. You're so much in love with that man it's ridiculous. He's gorgeous, he's nice, he's wonderful, and he obviously loves you."

"And he's running for state representative."

Maggie's eyes widened. "So what?"

"So what!" Lacey plunked the pitcher onto the counter beside her. "What would you do if the man you'd fallen for suddenly announced he wanted to become a rodeo cowboy?"

The light in Maggie's eyes slowly dimmed. "I'd run. As far and fast as I could. Oh, Lacey." She held out her arms.

Lacey went to her gladly, resting her head on Maggie's shoulder, fighting the sting of tears. "What am I going to do, Magoo?"

"I don't know, hon, I don't know."

Neither did Lacey.

When Clint came in that night for supper, Lacey steeled herself to act normal. She made it just fine—or as fine as she could—until she took him his apple pie for dessert. She placed the plate in front of him, but before she could withdraw, his fingers wrapped around her wrist.

Her knees went weak at the contact. "Let go," she whispered, her voice quivering.

"How long are you going to keep this up, Ruffles?"

She kept her gaze glued to his hand on her wrist. "I'm not trying to keep anything up. I'm just trying to get on with my life."

"Without me, right?"

There was pain underlying the harshness of his tone. Her eyes stung. "Clint, please. Let go." *Let go of my hand, let go of my heart.*

"You know I can't."

Her heart sped. Knowing she shouldn't, but unable to help herself, she looked into his eyes. It was almost her undoing. She didn't want to see his pain, his need. She had her own pain and need to deal with. But his deep blue eyes were filled with emotion. Pain and need . . . and, oh God, was that love?

No. It couldn't be. And even if it was, it didn't matter. There was no future for the two of them. Not if he intended to live his life in the public eye. With a low cry, she wrenched her wrist free and fled to the kitchen. She refused to go anywhere near him the rest of the night. When he went to the cash register to pay his check, she made Harriet go in her place.

Lacey barely slept at all that night. The next evening, she jumped every time the bell over the front door jingled. By eight o'clock he still hadn't shown, and her nerves were stretched to the point of screaming. By nine, she figured he wasn't coming and tried to relax. By nine thirty, she knew he wasn't. She told herself the lump in her throat was from relief, not disappointment.

It didn't matter. All that mattered was that he hadn't come. This was the first night since Clint had come to her apartment that he hadn't been in the café. As with her parents' absence, she should have been relieved. She wasn't. All she could do was wonder where he was, what he was doing. *Who he was with.*

The mere thought of him with another woman sent shards of agony through her heart.

He wouldn't. Surely he wouldn't turn to another woman so soon.

Why not? If you don't want him, why should he stay alone?

And it was Friday night. Date night. The night when everyone wanted to be with somebody, celebrate the end of the week, plan for the weekend.

At twenty past ten she told Mort good night and headed out the back door toward another night alone in her dingy apartment.

Stop feeling sorry for yourself. It's your own fault.

True, but what else could she do? She couldn't live with her mother's attitude. She couldn't deal with Clint's political aspirations.

Maybe he won't run for representative, a little voice whispered in her mind.

It was possible, wasn't it? He'd said he hadn't decided yet.

Something stabbed her palm. She looked down to find her hand on the splintery banister of the front stairs to her apartment. "That'll teach you to keep your mind on what you're doing," she whispered aloud.

The pain in her hand cleared her mind. Of course, Clint would run for representative. She was only kidding herself to think otherwise. The district needed someone like him, honest to a fault, hard working, with intimate, firsthand knowledge of the needs of the area. And if the paper was to be believed, Clint was the best, most logical, most popular choice for the job.

Every evening in the café she'd overheard people eagerly discussing next fall's election. The residents of Deep Fork wanted Clint to run. Wanted it wholeheartedly.

The least she could do, Lacey knew, would be to wish him well. She feared he'd need all the help he could get to survive in that nest of vipers known as the state legislature.

The mere thought of him being in the same building with Charles turned her blood cold.

Still, her mind wouldn't let go of the idea that Clint hadn't made his decision to run yet. The hope wouldn't die.

Until she saw his face a moment later, after she'd gone inside and turned on the lights and answered the knock on her door.

He stood there stiff and grim faced, his eyes bleak. "May I come in?"

When she hesitated, he said, "I won't stay long. There's something I need to tell you."

Lacey felt her stomach tighten. She knew by the look on his face what he would say. Still, she motioned him in.

He stopped just inside the door, making no move to come near her. He stuffed his fingers into his back pockets and looked her in the eye. "I've decided to run for state representative."

She looked away quickly. "I see."

"Do you?"

She forced herself to look back at him. "Yes, I do. The district needs a good representative. You'll be perfect for the job."

He eyed her carefully. "But?"

"No but. I mean it. I think you're the right man for the job." She swallowed and forced herself to go on. "I wish you all the best in your campaign. I know you'll win, and you'll be an excellent state representative."

He took a deep breath and dropped his hands to his sides. "I want you with me, Lacey."

Stunned, she could only stare at him, her heart racing with fear at the mere thought of going back to life in the public fishbowl. She shook her head. "You don't mean that."

"I do. You know it."

She couldn't hold his piercing gaze another instant. She turned away and wrapped her arms around her middle.

"No. I won't listen to this. It's over between us, Clint. It has to be."

An eternity of silence, broken only by a barking neighborhood dog somewhere outside, filled the room. Then Clint's voice came, soft and low and filled with regret. "I'm sorry you feel that way. I had thought . . . I thought we were pretty good together. Damn good, in fact. I guess that shows how wrong a man can be, wanting a woman, seeing visions of her in his grandmother's rocker—"

Lacey sucked in a breath. *Oh, God.*

"—wanting to marry her, raise a family."

Oh, God, oh God.

More silence stretched out. Lacey nearly screamed with the need to turn and throw herself into his arms. Instead, she clutched her sides harder and stood there, her back to him, and trembled.

Clint let out a sigh. "That's it then," he said. "You've obviously made up your mind. I won't bother you any more. Just remember one thing, though, will you? I love you. Guess I always will. Good-bye, Ruffles."

A moment later the door closed softly behind him. Lacey crumpled to the floor, shaken by silent sobs.

Clint leaned against the door frame and watched sheets of rain pour off his front porch roof. Too much rain, coming too fast for the gutters to handle. He tried not to remember the last time it had stormed, but couldn't help it.

Unbidden, the afternoon he and Lacey had gone to the farm for dinner with his folks came to mind. He remembered stopping on the way there to wipe off her lipstick and steal a kiss. He remembered the stinging jealousy he'd felt over Alex's attention to Lacey.

Then there had been that hour in her driveway, while the rain poured down. He remembered the way she tasted, the way she felt. Which led to other memories. Memories of their second trip to the farm together, when no one had been there. Just the two of them, and a fierce, uncontrollable passion like he'd never felt before.

He tipped his head back and closed his eyes. Why had he let her go so easily? He'd stood in that sorry excuse for an apartment behind the café—God, he couldn't stand to think of her living in such shabby surroundings—and let her end the best thing that had ever happened to him.

Let her, hell. He'd helped her. He hadn't argued against her half-baked reasoning. Hadn't tried to get to the real reason for her withdrawal from him.

Politics be damned. There was more to her fear than that. And fear it was, too. He'd seen it in her eyes. Fear of what, though? Him?

Maybe he'd pushed her too fast. Maybe she wasn't as ready as he was for the things he wanted, things he knew deep down she wanted too.

If he turned his head to the right even a fraction of an inch, he'd see his grandmother's rocking chair. Empty. But he couldn't look at it. Hadn't been able to look at it since that first night after he and Lacey had made love and she'd run from him.

She claimed they were finished; it was over between them. So why didn't he feel like it was over?

It wasn't over, dammit. Not for him. After what they had shared, the least she owed him was the truth. For whatever cold comfort that might give him.

Deep down, he didn't give a damn about the truth. He just wanted her back. In his arms, in his life. Where she belonged.

And he would get her back, too, he vowed.

Just as soon as he figured out how.

Charles. That was the key. She'd been fine until she learned Clint might run for state representative. She even said that was her reason for ending things between them. It had to have something to do with Charles, with the reason for their divorce.

She never had told him what had really happened between her and her ex, and he had asked her—twice. If

Clint were the suspicious type, he could almost believe she was hiding something. But if Charles had lied—and Clint firmly believed everything the man said had been a lie—then what was there to hide?

Hell. He could beat his head all night long and not come up with an answer. The only one around with answers was Lacey. And she didn't want anything to do with him.

"Or so she says," he told himself.

So far he had given her what she seemed to want—his absence from her life. He hadn't been in the café, hadn't seen her at all since a week ago last night, when he'd told her good-bye.

He still couldn't believe he'd done that. But at the time, all he had been able to think of was getting out of that dark, cramped room, getting away from her fast, before he made a complete fool of himself.

No more panic, no more fear, he decided. No more letting her evade the issue. Tomorrow was Sunday, her day off. He would find her and face her, force her to listen, to talk.

He shut the front door and went to stand before the rocker. "You'll sit in this chair, Ruffles," he said aloud. "You'll rock our babies in this chair. You want it as much as I do. Somehow, I'll make you see that."

Somehow.

"Well, damn." Lacey stared at the rip in the leg of her jeans and swallowed a scream. Screaming wouldn't help. Nothing would help. It was going to be another one of those days. Again.

Nothing seemed to have gone right for her since she came back to Deep Fork.

No, that wasn't exactly true, she admitted. Nothing had gone right for her in years. But coming home was supposed have made things better. Instead, she was now totally alienated from her parents, she'd fallen in love with a man she wasn't ready to love, didn't want to love—

don't think about it!—and she was completely, utterly, undeniably miserable.

Now her only clean pair of jeans sported a three-inch rip near the bottom hem of the right leg.

She glared at the rusty nail protruding from the third step from the top of her stairs. She'd been sidestepping it since the day she had moved into the garage apartment, meaning every day to find a hammer and remove the nail. But had she done it? Nooo. She'd put it off, played Scarlet O'Hara again, and told herself she'd think about it tomorrow.

The last time she had said that was yesterday. Now it was tomorrow. One day too late for her jeans. Her other pair was dirty. Maggie wasn't going to be home today for Lacey to use her washer and dryer, and the nearest laundromat was twenty miles away in Shawnee. That meant Lacey would have to go to her parents' house and finally get the rest of her clothes. Jeans were the standard work uniform at the café, and she would need a clean pair for tomorrow.

She looked at her watch. If she hurried, she could get to the house and be gone before her mother and father got home from church.

After pulling the hinged, barn-type doors open on the garage beneath her apartment, she started her car and backed out. Once on the street, the engine set up an ominous clatter. Lacey clenched her fingers around the steering wheel. The car wasn't going to last much longer. How was she going to attend college in Shawnee without a car?

While Mort and Maggie wouldn't hear of accepting rent money from Lacey for the old garage apartment, she certainly didn't earn enough at the café to buy a car and commute. If she moved to Shawnee and got a better-paying job, she would have to pay rent. She didn't have the kinds of skills required to earn enough for rent, utilities, car payment, tuition, books . . . the list of expenses would be endless. It would be tough to even find a job in Shawnee. The city had two colleges. Students from both campuses competed fiercely for the few jobs available.

With her car acting up, and the likelihood that Donna Hazelwood would want her job back at the café in a few weeks, Lacey's options were dwindling.

It was five 'til twelve. The way things were going, she fully expected the preacher to have ended his sermon early for the first time in history and to find her parents already home from church.

This time, however, luck was with her. She figured she had just enough time to run in, grab the rest of her clothing, and get away before her mother and father came home.

When she pulled into the driveway, she spotted Clint's pickup next door. A lump rose in her throat. She missed him. Oh, how she missed him.

She had lain awake night after night, wondering if she was doing the right thing in pushing him away. Then he had mentioned marriage, and she'd known. If he was serious about a career in state politics, the best thing she could do for him would be to stay as far away as possible.

But God, how it hurt. His smile came to her at night, haunting her, teasing her. Sometimes she woke and thought she heard his laughter, or felt his touch.

With a curse, she killed the engine and got out of the car. If she didn't stop thinking about Clint soon, she would go crazy. And if she kept dawdling in the driveway, her parents would be here before she left.

She let herself in the front door and went straight to her old room. She was on her knees, pulling jeans out of the bottom dresser drawer, when she heard the hall floor creak.

"Hello, Lacey."

At the sound of Clint's voice she froze, her back to the door. God, what was he doing here? Why couldn't he just stay away? Slowly, knowing she shouldn't, she turned to face him.

He looked about like she felt. Dark circles hung beneath

sunken eyes. The hollows in his cheeks were more pronounced. He'd lost weight.

She fought the sting of tears. "What do you want?"

He came and knelt beside her, then took her face in his hands. Before she could pull away, he whispered, "This," and kissed her.

A violent shudder ripped through her. The tears she fought sprung loose. She tore her lips from his. "No," she cried. She turned away and hugged herself, bending over against the pain of denying him. "No."

From behind, his arms came around her. He leaned his chest against her back. "Yes, Lacey, yes. Talk to me. Tell me what's wrong. I know there's more to it than just my running for office."

"Don't be too sure about that, Clint."

Lacey and Clint both jerked at the sound of her mother's voice from the doorway. Lacey groaned. This couldn't be happening.

Behind her, Clint stood, then helped her rise. He faced her mother, while Lacey refused to.

"You're the one who thinks Charles lied," Irma said to Clint. "Of course, she doesn't want you going to work in the same building with her husband."

Lacey whipped her head around and glared. "*Ex*-husband."

Irma went on as though Lacey hadn't spoken. "She wouldn't want that at all. If you were around Charles very often, she's probably afraid you'll realize a man like him couldn't lie. Not about his own wife."

"Mrs. H.—"

"Save it, Clint," Lacey said. "She wouldn't know the truth if it jumped up and bit her. She wouldn't recognize a lie if it stared her in the face."

"Watch your tongue, girl. I know a lie when I hear one."

"No, you don't, Mama. You never dreamed of questioning his lies about where I was those weekends before I left him. You didn't recognize it for a lie when he told you *I* was the one who didn't want children. You didn't recognize the lie about me being the one to insist on spending all our holidays with his family instead of with you.''

Irma gaped. ''If those were lies, why didn't you say something?''

''Say something?'' Lacey cried, outraged. ''I stood right there in the kitchen and told you—''

''No, not about the weekends,'' Irma said with a wave of her hand. ''About the other.''

''He was my husband, Mama,'' Lacey wailed. ''When the lies started, I didn't understand what was happening. What was I supposed to do, start an argument with him in front of you? I was embarrassed to have you think badly of him. I wanted you to like him.''

Neal had come to stand at Irma's shoulders. He shook his head. ''I don't understand any of this. It might make sense to think he lied about those things because the lies made him look good. But this other, about your divorce . . . He wouldn't have lied about his wife running around with other men. A man wouldn't purposefully make himself look like a fool.''

Lacey didn't stop to think. She only knew the unbearable tension inside her had gone on too long. ''I'm only going to say this once, so you'd better listen. Charles and I did not get divorced because I slept with other men. We got divorced because I *refused* to sleep with other men.''

The quiet that followed Lacey's words was absolute.

Lacey could have bitten off her tongue. She wanted to call the humiliating words back and bury them so deep they could never get out. The mere idea that her own husband, the man she had loved, had been married to for ten years, could ask—no, *demand*—such a thing from her made her want to die. She squeezed her eyes shut.

Then the room came to life. ''He wouldn't!'' Irma cried.

''He damn sure better not have,'' Clint said with a

growl. He turned her toward him and held both her shoulders. "What happened?"

Something in his voice made her look at him. While his touch was gentle, his face was filled with horror, and something else she wasn't sure of.

"Why would he want you to do such a thing?" Clint demanded.

Lacey felt sick. She knew she couldn't drop a bomb like that without explaining. It took her a long moment to swallow the bile and force the words out. But she couldn't look at Clint, not even her parents, so she closed her eyes again.

"He had a bill in committee. It was about to die. He made a deal with the committee chair. Seems the man . . . liked me."

Clint's fingers dug into her shoulders, and that other look in his eyes flamed and identified itself. Rage. "Damn that bastard!" Pure, unadulterated rage. "Is this why you've stayed away from me since you heard I might run for office? You think I'd end up doing something like that to you?"

"No! Good God, no, Clint, never! I never thought it!"

"Thank heaven." Disregarding her parents still standing in the doorway, Clint pulled Lacey to his chest and wrapped his arms around her. "Ah, hell, Ruffles, why didn't you tell me what he'd done to you?"

Heaven help her, her cheeks were wet. She couldn't talk for trying to stem the tears.

"Why, Ruffles? Why wouldn't you tell me when I asked?"

"Because I can't even bear to think about it," she cried. "It makes me feel . . . dirty."

"No! No, not you. *Him.* He's the one who should feel that way, not you." Clint held her away and wiped her cheeks with his thumbs. "But don't you see? There's nothing to keep us apart, Ruffles. I won't let him hurt you anymore."

Lacey blinked. "Me? You think I've been worried

about me? It's you," she cried. "You can't work in the same building with him, you can't even run for election if you have anything to do with me. The minute he hears my name connected with yours, he'll ruin you. He'll spread more lies and rumors, he'll discredit you any way he can, don't you see?"

"He won't," Clint said fiercely. "He can't. All it takes is one word in his ear, and he'll clam up so tight you'll never hear another peep out of the sorry bastard."

"No." She stepped away from his hold. "You don't know him like I do. He's desperate. That's why he came here with his lies in the first place. If I told anyone what he'd done, if anybody believed me, he would be ruined. His career would be over. He's *desperate*, I tell you. He'll do anything to discredit me and anyone associated with me."

The rage drained from Clint's face. Something softer took its place. "This is why you said you wouldn't see me any more? Why you wouldn't marry me?"

Twin gasps came from the doorway. Lacey ignored them. Damn, her nose was going to run. She sniffed. "Yes."

Clint smiled, one of those sexy, breathtaking smiles that made her knees weak. "If I ever needed proof, I guess you just gave it to me."

"Proof of what?" she said irritably. How could he look so happy, damn him, when her whole world was crashing down?

"Proof of how much you love me." His smile faded. "I know you think this is all for my own good, Lacey, but it isn't necessary. We don't have to give up anything. His lies and rumors can't hurt me, and they're easy enough to stop." He smiled again. "So what do you say? Marry me?"

Aching inside, wanting to say yes, wanting to shout it, Lacey forced herself to take another step away. He didn't understand how vicious Charles could be, how powerful he'd become. Charles could utterly *destroy* an honest man like Clint.

"No," she whispered. "You haven't been listening to me. I can't have anything to do with you. I won't be responsible for all the terrible things that could happen. I won't, I tell you!"

Before anyone could stop her, she barrelled past her parents and fled.

FIFTEEN

Clint started to run after Lacey, but Mrs. H. stopped him. "Let her go, son."

He wanted to argue, to pull free of her grasp.

Mr. H. spoke up. "She's right, Clint, let her go. Give her a little time. We've all . . . put her through a lot these past weeks. Let her calm down some."

"She's hurting," Clint protested. "I can't let her hurt like that because of that worthless jackass she married."

"Yes, you can," Mrs. H. said firmly. "If what she said was the truth—"

"If? *If?*" Clint was appalled. "You mean you still don't believe her?"

"Think, Clint," Mrs. H. urged. "If Charles really was lying, if Lacey didn't run off with another man, then where in the world did she go for six whole months? Why didn't she come home?"

"Come home to what?" Clint jerked free of her grasp. "To parents who don't believe a word she says? People who are so enamored of their rich, powerful son-in-law that they take his word over that of their own daughter? No wonder she went to stay at her cousin's."

Mrs. H.'s eyes widened. "Her . . . cousin?"

"The one in California. Lacey house-sat for her."

"Oh." Before his eyes, Mrs. H. seemed to shrink and age. "Oh, my. Oh, Clint! You have to go after her."

"I plan to." Clint started for the door.

"Tell her . . ."

Clint paused in the hall.

"Tell her . . . we're sorry. Tell her . . . we love her."

Clint gave a wry grin. "I'll tell her, but she's going to need to hear it from you."

With that, he decided he'd wasted too much time. He dashed out of the house. As expected, Lacey's car was gone. Deep Fork was a small town. She couldn't have gone far. He would start with her apartment.

When he got there, he at first thought she wasn't home. He knocked, but she didn't answer. He knocked again, louder. Still no answer, but a sixth sense told him she was inside.

"Lacey, open the door."

Nothing.

He pounded again. "I'm not going away, Lacey. Open the door. The neighbors are starting to stare."

Still nothing. He pounded harder. He kept pounding until long after his fist went numb. Just when he was about to give up, the door flew open.

"What the hell do you think you're doing?" Lacey cried. "Go away and leave me—"

Instead of letting her finish, Clint pushed his way inside. "Not on your life, lady. Not until you tell me the real reason you don't want to be around me. I think I deserve that much."

"I've told you the reason," she cried.

Clint had intended to soothe her, ease her pain, not storm in the door yelling at her. But dammit, she frustrated the hell out of him. He took a deep breath and tried to calm himself.

"I love you," he told her. "And you love me. What could be more important than our being together?"

She looked away sharply. "I never said I loved you."

He almost flinched. But he wouldn't let her know how

much her words hurt. "No, you never said it. But it's true. We both know it."

"It doesn't matter who does or doesn't love whom. If you don't stay away from me when you run for election, you'll learn to hate me soon enough. Charles will see to that."

"Damn Charles!" Something inside Clint snapped. "And damn you. Do you ever think about anything but him?"

Lacey backed away, her eyes wide and tear filled. But Clint couldn't stop.

"Maybe you're right," he said, unable to keep the emotion from his voice. "Maybe we don't belong together. If Charles has still got this big an influence over you, you might as well go back to the son of a bitch. If you ever decide to kick him out of your life, let me know. Until then, forget it. I never did like triangles."

Lacey reeled as though Clint had slapped her. When she blinked to clear her vision, he was gone. Gone for good, this time. She knew it. He wouldn't be back.

Violent tremors shook her. She made it to the couch, where she sat staring at the blank wall, clutching her icy hands together.

Clint's gone.

The thought rang over and over in her mind.

Clint's gone.

But isn't that what you wanted?

No! Not like this. Not with him hating me.

What was she going to do?

Nothing. It's done.

Done. What a final word. She had wanted to end her involvement with Clint, and she had. And then some. The old saying about being careful what you wish for played through her mind during the next few days.

There was no help for it. Clint was out of her life. She was on her own. She had come back to Deep Fork so she could get her business degree. It was time, as her father would say, "to fish or cut bait."

* * *

Apparently her parents still had their doubts about her, Lacey thought, because she hadn't heard from either of them since Sunday. "They're cutting me loose," she said.

Maggie pulled the last two pairs of jeans from the dryer. "Bull hockey." She tossed the size three Lee Riders to Lacey, then folded the size eight Wranglers and added them to her own pile. "They're just waiting for you to make the next move."

"What move is that? When I move clear out of town?"

It was Lacey's day off, and she'd brought her dirty laundry to Maggie's. Between the wash cycle and the final rinse, Lacey had finally told her the entire story.

"Don't be silly," Maggie said. "Out of town, indeed."

"Well it seems to me, if I made the last move, they should make the next one."

"Your parents are going to be a little slow doing that, I imagine. They know now how wrong they've been. My guess is they're waiting for you to forgive them. Clint's just waiting for you to come to your senses."

Lacey shook her head. "I *have* come to my senses. I'm right to call it quits between us. I won't be responsible for the destruction of his future political career."

"You're that powerful, are you?"

Stung by Maggie's tone, Lacey said, "Not me, Charles."

"He's that powerful?"

"He's that . . . mean, that vicious. That determined to protect himself at all costs, no matter who gets in his way."

"And you told all this to Clint?"

"Of course I did. I was trying to make him understand why he can't have anything to do with me if he runs for election."

Maggie dropped to the chair beside her. "You *said* all this to Clint?"

Puzzled at Maggie's tone, hurt that her best friend wasn't being more sympathetic, Lacey nodded.

"No wonder he blew up the way he did. I can't believe you would insult Clint Sutherland like that."

"Insult? I haven't insulted him."

"You haven't—? Good gracious! You've just told him he's not smart enough or strong enough to deal with a sewer rat like Charles Johnston. If that's not an insult, I don't know what is."

"Oh, come on, Maggie—"

"No, you come on. Clint was right. When are you going to stop giving that creep you married complete control over your life?"

A cold shiver ran down Lacey's spine. "What are you talking about?"

"Think back, Lacey. From the minute you quit school ten years ago so you could work two jobs putting him through law school, Charles has called all the shots. Everything you've done has been for him, because of him. You let him—no, *helped* him lie to your parents for years. You put up with him. You're close to thirty years old and haven't started a family because he didn't want the responsibility."

"That's ancient history. I had no business having children if my husband didn't want them."

"True. But instead of standing up to him last fall when all this happened, instead of telling the world what kind of monster he really is, you let him have his way when you ran off and hid. Now, you're still letting him have his way. You're willing to let him go on making you out to be the tramp of the century, and for what?"

All Lacey could do was stare at Maggie.

"I'll tell you for what," Maggie said fiercely. "Because you're so used to knuckling under, to letting him have his way, to living with pain and disillusionment, it's become a habit with you. You'd rather go on the way you are now than expend the energy to learn how to stand on your own two feet."

Lacey pressed her fingertips to her temples. "I'm *trying*

to stand on my own two feet, dammit. That's one reason why I can't get involved with Clint.''

"What the devil does that have to do with anything?''

"It has everything to do with it. How can I stand on my own two feet if I turn right around and give Clint the same power over me Charles had?''

"You,'' Maggie said, pointing a finger, "are one mixed up lady. Loving a man, marrying him, doesn't mean lying down and turning yourself into a doormat, the way you did for Charles. Do you honestly think Clint would expect that of you? Would even allow it? You don't have to stand three paces behind, dammit. When you love a man, and he loves you, you stand *beside* each other. You make decisions *together*. You don't let him have his way all the time, unless he wants the same things you do.''

Maggie threw her hands in the air. "Hell, I don't know why I'm wasting my breath. You're a big girl, Lacey. It's time you gave a long, hard look at yourself and decided if you're grown up enough to stand up for yourself, to take what you want out of life.''

The words hurt. All the more because Lacey feared they were true. She shook her head. "Maybe you're right, but what am I supposed to do? How do I keep myself from falling into the same trap with Clint?''

"You don't see it, do you?''

"See what?''

"The difference, dammit. When you fell for Charles, you were young and impressionable. You thought he was a god. You worshiped him.''

Lacey gave a half smile. "Yeah, I guess.''

"I'd bet the farm that's not how you feel about Clint. You're no starry-eyed teenager out in the world for the first time. And he's no god, he's a flesh and blood man. When he hurt you, you lashed back. You didn't crawl into a corner and let him get away with it. You're growing up, Lacey. We all do. You can handle it, I know you can.''

*   *   *

Maggie's words played over and over in Lacey's mind all that night and the next day, and something strange happened. Lacey could actually feel herself growing up. She felt as though maybe, just maybe, if she took things one step at a time, she could have what she wanted from life. If she tried hard enough. And if she had just a little bit of luck.

As if in answer to a prayer, the luck she needed came almost instantly. Friday afternoon Maggie let her know that Donna had decided to stay home with the new baby rather than come back to work. If Lacey wanted to stay on at the café, the job was hers. And Maggie and Mort both insisted that the garage apartment be part of her wage.

Lacey didn't argue with them. She would take the offer and build on it. With a permanent job and no rent to pay, she just might, *might* be able to enroll in college next fall. If she could avoid spending every cent she made just to keep her car running.

And what about Clint? the little voice in her head asked.

Lacey had no answer. Had she really hurt him the way Maggie said? If so, would he even want her now?

Just as important, Lacey had to settle something in her own mind. She had to decide if she was mature enough to stand beside a man like Clint. An honest, hardworking man. He wouldn't want a doormat, and Lord knew, she didn't want to be one, not ever again.

Clint deserved a partner. A lifetime partner who would stand beside him, have his children, bully him when he deserved it, love him when he didn't. He needed the best.

She just wasn't certain she was up to the challenge.

Nor was she sure she was up to the challenge of what to do about her parents. They had made no effort to contact her, and it had been nearly a week since she had run out of their house in tears. Did that mean they still didn't believe her? Or was Maggie right, and were they waiting for her to forgive them?

If so, the next question she faced was *could* she forgive

them. The things they had put her through—especially her mother, but her father had stood by and watched, so he, too, was to blame—were still so fresh. The pain, the heartache, the humiliation of being called a liar by her own mother.

Heaven help her, she didn't know what to do.

She hadn't reached any decision by the time her hand was forced. Friday night her father came to the café. He took a seat in her section. Just the sight of him stirred all the animosity she'd tried to hold in check for weeks.

But there was also another stirring deep down. The stirring of memories, of a little girl who loved her daddy.

Torn, not knowing what else to do, she took him a glass of water and a dinner menu.

When he gave her that hang-dog look of his, she didn't know whether to hug him or dump the water on his head.

"How's my sugarpie?" he asked.

Lacey bit the inside of her cheek.

When she didn't answer, he asked, "Did, uh, did Clint give you our message?"

Just the mention of Clint's name sent a fresh pain knifing through her stomach. She shook her head. "What message?"

Her father reached out as if to take her hand, then stopped. "We asked him, that is, your mother and I wanted . . . wanted him to tell you how sorry we are. About everything. We love you, Lacey June."

Lacey felt her eyes burn.

"If you're free tomorrow morning, could you . . . come home and . . . talk to us? We need to talk, Lacey. We can't let this stand between us."

Lacey studied his workworn hand where it lay on the Formica table. He was right. They needed to talk. What she would find to say to them, she didn't know, but Saturday morning she found herself walking up their sidewalk.

Her parents greeted her at the door with tears and open arms. "Oh, honey," her mother cried.

Neal put his arms around both women and hugged them

tight. "It's all right now. It's all behind us. Everything's going to be fine."

Irma stepped back and dried her eyes. "Nothing will be fine until I've had my say." She looked at Lacey and her eyes watered again. "I've been doing a lot of thinking since Sunday."

"Me, too," Lacey admitted.

"I know how wrong I was to believe Charles. We were fools, honey. That's all there is to it." Irma took a deep breath. "There. I feel much better."

Lacey stared at her beaming parents, amazed. "That's it?" she asked. "That's all either of you have to say?"

A look of uncertainty crossed their faces.

"We're sorry, honey," Irma said. "We know we hurt you, but it's over. You can move back home now. You'll see, everything will be fine."

"Fine?" Lacey cried. "After what you've put me through, you expect me to just come home like it was *nothing?* A simple, 'We're sorry,' and that's it?"

"Of course, we're sorry," Irma said earnestly. "We were wrong not to believe in you. We love you. Can't you forgive us?"

Forgive them? Could she?

More importantly, could she not?

Her head swam; her stomach ached. "You *hurt* me, dammit. I can't just smile and pretend it never happened, the way you apparently can."

"Maybe," her father said tentatively, "maybe after you move back home, you'll—"

"I'm not moving back home. I should never have come here in the first place."

"But . . . what will you do?"

Poor Mama, Lacey thought. *She looks so bewildered.*

"I plan to stay in my apartment, work at the café, and see about financial aid for going back to college."

Her father placed a hand on her mother's shoulder. "Does this mean," he asked Lacey, "that you . . . don't want to see us anymore? Have we hurt you that badly?"

Damn. Why was this so hard?

"Yes," she told him. "You hurt me that badly. But it doesn't mean I don't ever want to see you again. You're just going to have to give me a little time to heal."

"We can do that, honey." Irma took Lacey's hand in hers, and Lacey let her. "You take all the time you need. I guess you've got some pretty deep wounds. Just don't . . . don't stop loving us, Lacey."

Lacey's vision blurred. "You, too, Mama." She squeezed her mother's hand. "I've got to go now. I'll see you later."

Lacey thought about her parents the rest of the morning and into the afternoon. She thought about them when she went to work. Thought about them so much she had trouble remembering which order went with which customer.

All she needed to make her disastrous week complete was for Clint to come into the café and sit where she would have to wait on him.

Clint, with his hot blue eyes, his sexy, bone-melting smile. Her fingers remembered the feel of this thick, silky hair, of the hard muscles in his arms and back. Her lips remembered the taste of his. Her heart remembered the rhythm of his, as the two of them had lain heart to heart and loved each other.

She remembered the sound of his laughter in the darkness, the warm feeling of knowing he was near, the pleasure of his teasing, the way his voice went rough and tender when he called her Ruffles.

Heaven help her, the water in the glasses on the tray she carried was sloshing. She set the tray down on the counter and wiped her palms against her thighs.

It was time. Right here, and right now, she had to decide once and for all if she was adult enough, *woman* enough, to grab for the life she wanted.

Maybe what she really should worry about was, did she deserve the things she wanted.

Bull hockey. That's what Maggie would say to such a question.

Everyone made mistakes, and Lacey had made some doozies. First with Charles, then Clint.

That growing-up feeling came over her again.

Of course, she had made mistakes, but she damn well didn't intend to beat her chest over them the rest of her life.

And if she wasn't woman enough for Clint Sutherland, nobody was, by damn.

Then another question gave her pause. Was she mature enough to make peace with her parents?

It was time to find out. Neglecting the customers waiting for their water, Lacey dug into her pocket for change and went to the pay phone.

"Mama? Can you come to the café? I'd like to see you and daddy."

"Oh, honey." Irma paused and sniffed. "We'll be right there."

Within ten minutes, Lacey's parents walked through the door of the café. Lacey met them before they reached a table. Her heart melted at their hopeful expressions. They wanted her forgiveness. It was plain in their eyes.

Lacey learned something then and there about love that she had never realized. When someone loved you, they not only gave you their heart, they also gave you the power to hurt them.

If she hadn't loved them so much, her parents' lack of faith in her wouldn't have nearly crippled her.

If she hadn't loved Clint, he, too, could not have hurt her. And if he hadn't loved her, she . . . oh, Lord, how she had hurt him.

She knew, in that instant, that she had the power to inflict that same fierce pain on both her parents. All she had to do was withhold that which she knew they wanted most—her forgiveness.

But there was no question in her mind as to what she

would do. She didn't have the stomach or the heart for petty spite.

She opened her eyes. "Mama, Daddy, I love you."

Clint checked all the doors one last time, then went out the front door and locked it behind him. When he saw Lacey leaning against the loading dock, he didn't bat an eye. He'd seen her face so often in his mind in the past weeks, seen her so many times in his dreams, he almost walked right past her before a whiff of familiar perfume told him she was really there.

He stopped dead in his tracks. "What are you doing here?" If she answered, he'd know he wasn't dreaming.

She gave him a shrug. "Thought I'd walk you home, if it's all right."

Clint frowned. Was she here to reinforce her reasons for rejecting him? Would she tell him again how he wasn't strong enough or smart enough to deal with her ex-husband?

In reality, he didn't think he cared if she did those things or not. As long as he could be near her, see her, maybe, if he was careful, even touch her. But he couldn't let her see how desperate he was for just the sound of her voice.

He shrugged back at her. "Suit yourself."

With every step they took, he wondered why she was there, what she wanted. He was afraid to ask.

Afraid?

Yeah, okay, he could admit that.

He was afraid to know she wanted nothing more than a walk down the street. He was afraid she would look at him and see into his soul, see how much he wanted her, loved her. That she would once again throw it back in his face.

She had needed him after that scene last week with her parents. Needed his support, his understanding. And what had he done? Fool that he was, he'd let his feelings get hurt and had lashed out at her, walked out on her.

Maybe she had come to tell him good-bye.

They turned the corner at his street and started up the sidewalk. He couldn't stand the silence. "Did you quit your job?" he asked without looking at her.

"No. Matter of fact, it's permanent now. Donna's decided to stay home with the baby."

At his front porch, Clint took her arm and made her face him. "Why are you here instead of at work?"

Lacey gave a nonchalant shrug. "Mama's decided to try her hand at waitressing."

Clint blinked. "Your mother is waiting tables? Why?"

"I wanted some time off." She cocked her head. "Are you going to invite me inside?"

Was that uncertainty he saw in her eyes? He couldn't be sure. His heart didn't care, all it wanted to do was pound. "Inside. Sure." He opened the door and followed her in. He couldn't think of what to say to her. "Can I get you something to drink?" Brilliant.

She gave him a little half smile. "No, thanks."

The look on her face, the way she flexed and unflexed her fingers—oh God, her nails were red again—gave him the impression she was nervous. That was understandable, he supposed. Their last parting had been rather . . . emotional.

"Why are you here, Lacey?"

Lacey breathed deeply, praying for courage. "To . . . to tell you you were right."

"About what?"

"A lot of things. About how much influence I let Charles have over me, even after I left him. I wanted you to know . . . that's all over now. I'm standing on my own two feet these days. I even applied for a grant for college. I've made peace with my parents." It was amazing how fast courage could flee.

She took another deep breath. "My life is almost just the way I want it."

"Almost?"

Lacey's nerve nearly fled. Surely he knew what she was

trying to say, but he wasn't going to make it easy on her. She guessed she couldn't blame him for that.

"Lacey?"

She hadn't realized how much time she'd taken. "I, uh . . ." Lord, this was hard. She glanced around the room, desperately seeking something, anything to help her. And there it stood. All the help she could have asked for. Help from generations of Sutherland women.

She walked over to the old rocker and rested her hand along the polished back. "You . . . made me an offer not long ago." She had to stop and swallow, afraid to look him in the eye. Instead, she stared at his knees. "It had to do with this chair."

When he came and stood only inches away, her heart threatened to beat its way right up her throat. Slowly, against her will, her gaze traveled up to meet his.

"I remember," he whispered. His Adam's apple bobbed up and down.

She waited, but he said nothing more. It was up to her, then. Stalling, she looked away and ran a finger over the curved scrollwork on the back of the chair. She raised her gaze to his again. "Is the offer . . . still open?"

Something flared in his eyes. Something hot, something painful. "That depends."

Lacey felt her hands tremble. He was supposed to say yes, not *that depends*. "Depends on what?"

He stared at her a long moment, scorched her, took her breath away with those flaming blue eyes. Then he reached for her. "Sit down." He guided her into the rocker.

The hard cherrywood hugged her, welcomed her, curved and dipped, fitting her body as though it were made for her. As she looked up at Clint, her eyes filled.

"It fits you," he said, his voice rusty.

"Yes."

He knelt before her and took both her hands. Softly, solemnly, he said, "I love you, Ruffles."

She gripped his fingers and felt her tears spill over. "And I love you, Clint Sutherland, with all my heart."

He let out a breath she hadn't known he was holding, and dropped his head to her lap. "Then for God's sake," came his tortured whisper, "marry me. Work in the café if you want. Go to school and get your degree, start your own business. Climb mountains. Anything you want. But marry me. And when the time comes . . . when you're ready . . ." He raised his head, and she bit back a cry. His beautiful blue eyes were swimming.

"When you're ready," he said, his voice rough with emotion, "let me give you the babies you've always wanted."

"*Yes*." She lowered her head to his and tracked tears and fevered kisses across his lips, making him shiver. "Yes, yes, yes!"

SHARE THE FUN . . .
SHARE YOUR NEW-FOUND TREASURE!!

You don't want to let your new books out of your sight?
That's okay. Your friends can get their own. Order below.

No. 65 TO CATCH A LORELEI by Phyllis Houseman
Lorelei sets a trap for Daniel but gets caught in it herself.

No. 66 BACK OF BEYOND by Shirley Faye
Dani and Jesse are forced to face their true feelings for each other.

No. 67 CRYSTAL CLEAR by Cay David
Max could be the end of all Crystal's dreams . . . or just the beginning!

No. 68 PROMISE OF PARADISE by Karen Lawton Barrett
Gabriel is surprised to find that Eden's beauty is not just skin deep.

No. 69 OCEAN OF DREAMS by Patricia Hagan
Is Jenny just another shipboard romance to Officer Kirk Moen?

No. 70 SUNDAY KIND OF LOVE by Lois Faye Dyer
Trace literally sweeps beautiful, ebony-haired Lily off her feet.

No. 71 ISLAND SECRETS by Darcy Rice
Chad has the power to take away Tucker's hard-earned independence.

No. 72 COMING HOME by Janis Reams Hudson
Clint always loved Lacey. Now Fate has given them another chance.
